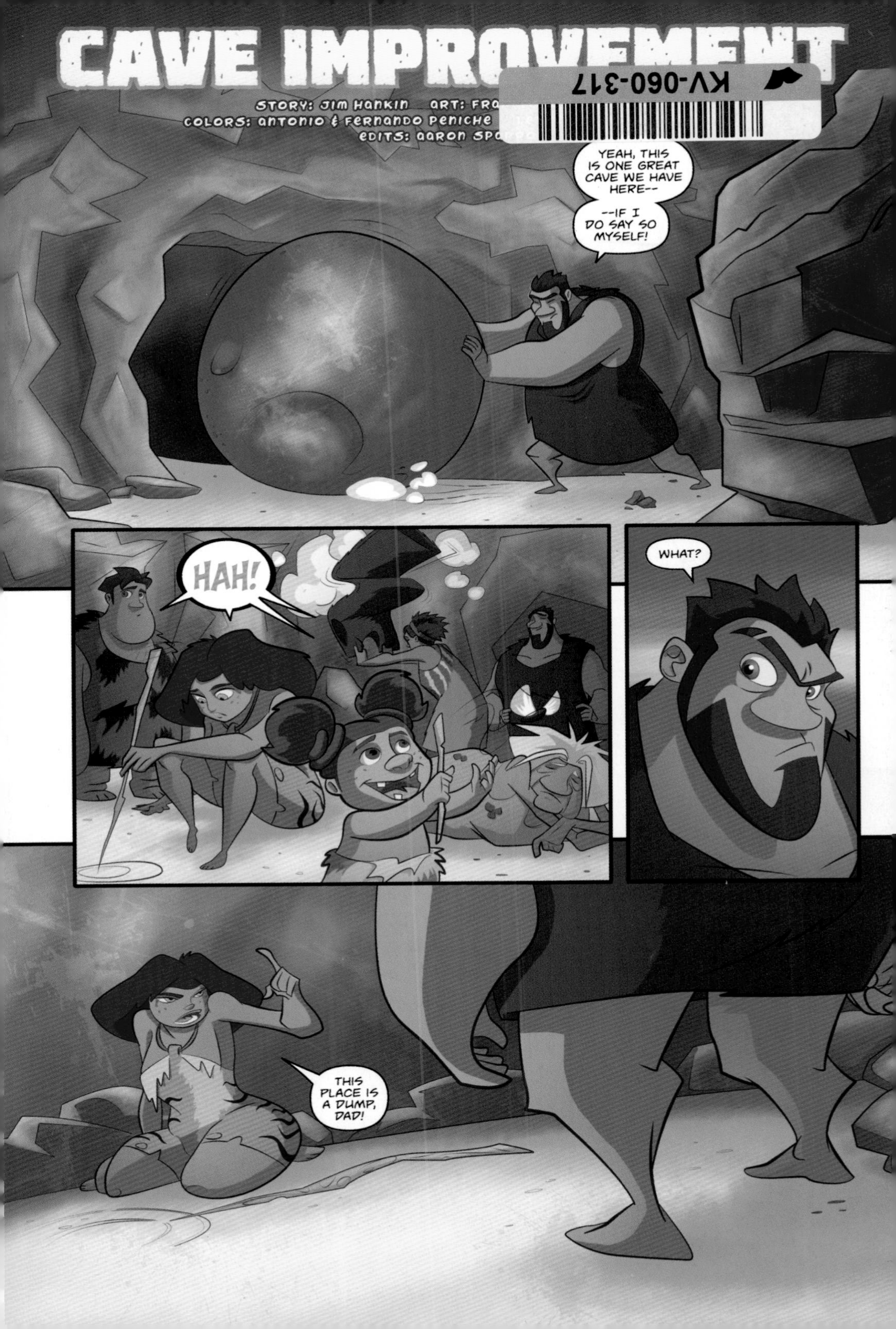
CAVE IMPROVEMENT
STORY: JIM HANKIN ART:
COLORS: ANTONIO & FERNANDO PENICHE
EDITS: AARON
YEAH, THIS IS ONE GREAT CAVE WE HAVE HERE--
--IF I DO SAY SO MYSELF!
HAH!
WHAT?
THIS PLACE IS A DUMP, DAD!

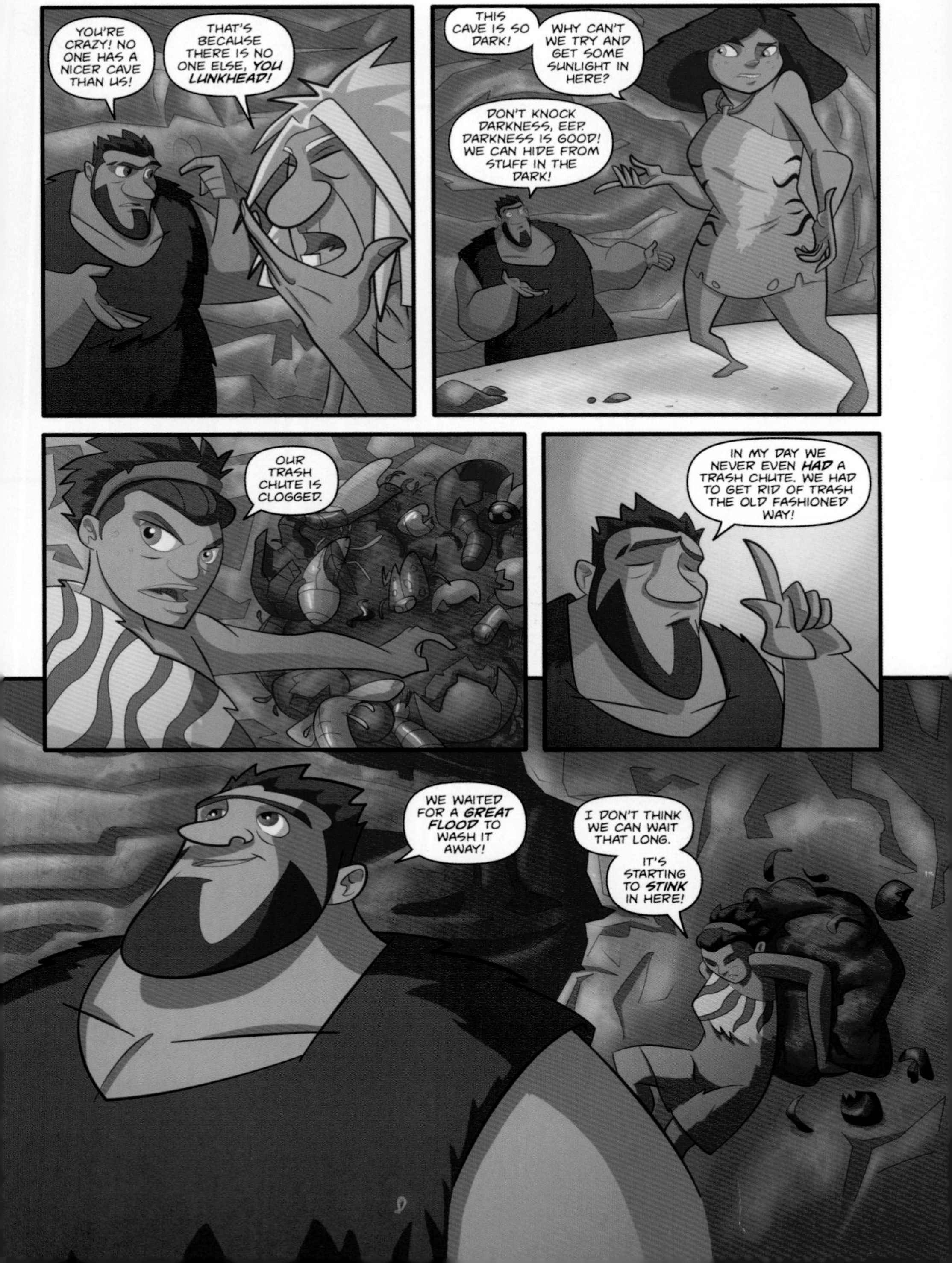

YOU'RE CRAZY! NO ONE HAS A NICER CAVE THAN US!
THAT'S BECAUSE THERE IS NO ONE ELSE, YOU LUNKHEAD!
THIS CAVE IS SO DARK!
WHY CAN'T WE TRY AND GET SOME SUNLIGHT IN HERE?
DON'T KNOCK DARKNESS, EEP. DARKNESS IS GOOD! WE CAN HIDE FROM STUFF IN THE DARK!
OUR TRASH CHUTE IS CLOGGED.
IN MY DAY WE NEVER EVEN HAD A TRASH CHUTE. WE HAD TO GET RID OF TRASH THE OLD FASHIONED WAY!
WE WAITED FOR A GREAT FLOOD TO WASH IT AWAY!
I DON'T THINK WE CAN WAIT THAT LONG.
IT'S STARTING TO STINK IN HERE!

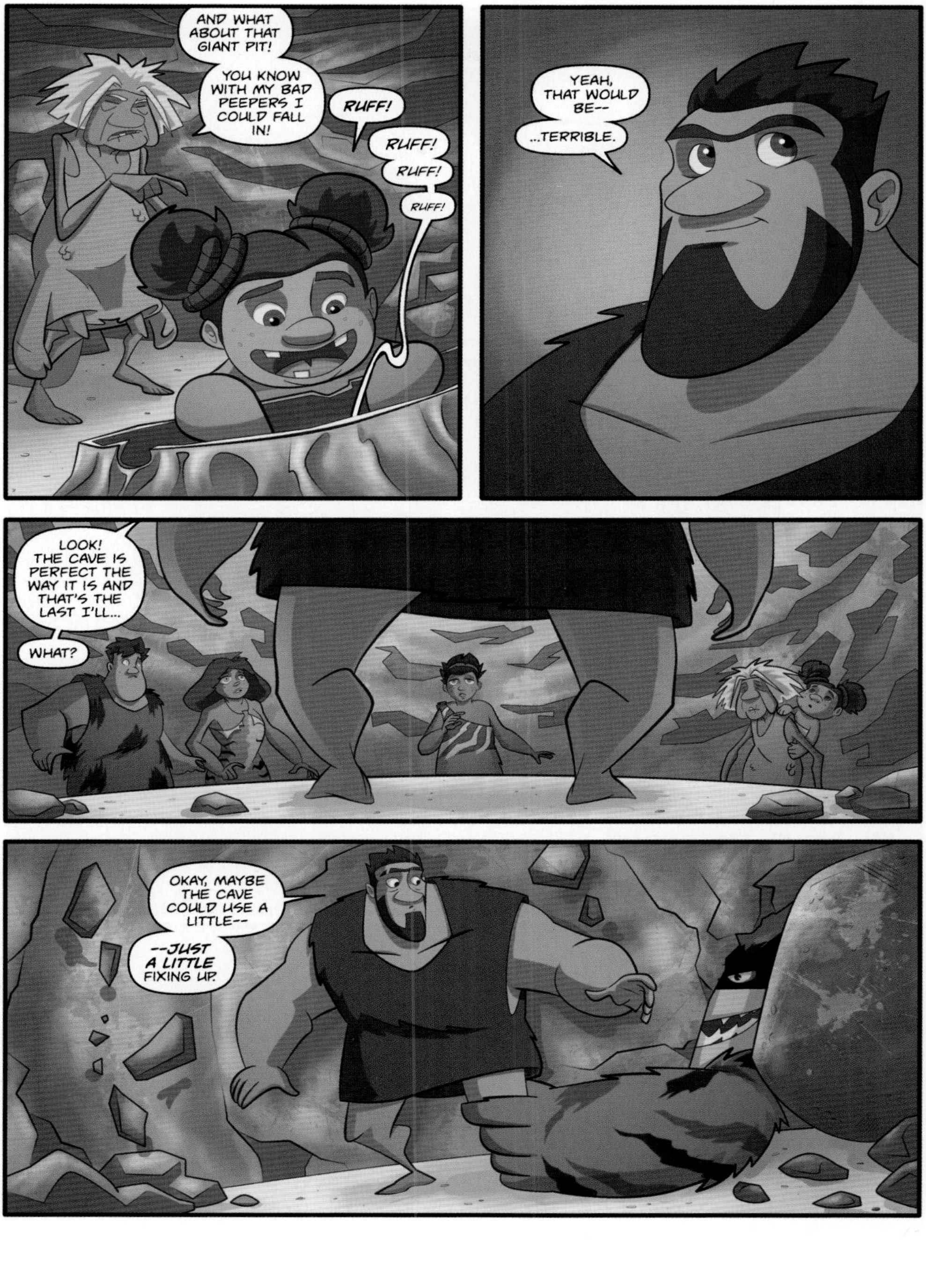
AND WHAT ABOUT THAT GIANT PIT!
YOU KNOW WITH MY BAD PEEPERS I COULD FALL IN!
RUFF!
RUFF!
RUFF!
RUFF!
YEAH, THAT WOULD BE--
...TERRIBLE.
LOOK! THE CAVE IS PERFECT THE WAY IT IS AND THAT'S THE LAST I'LL...
WHAT?
OKAY, MAYBE THE CAVE COULD USE A LITTLE--
--JUST A LITTLE FIXING UP.

The next morning...

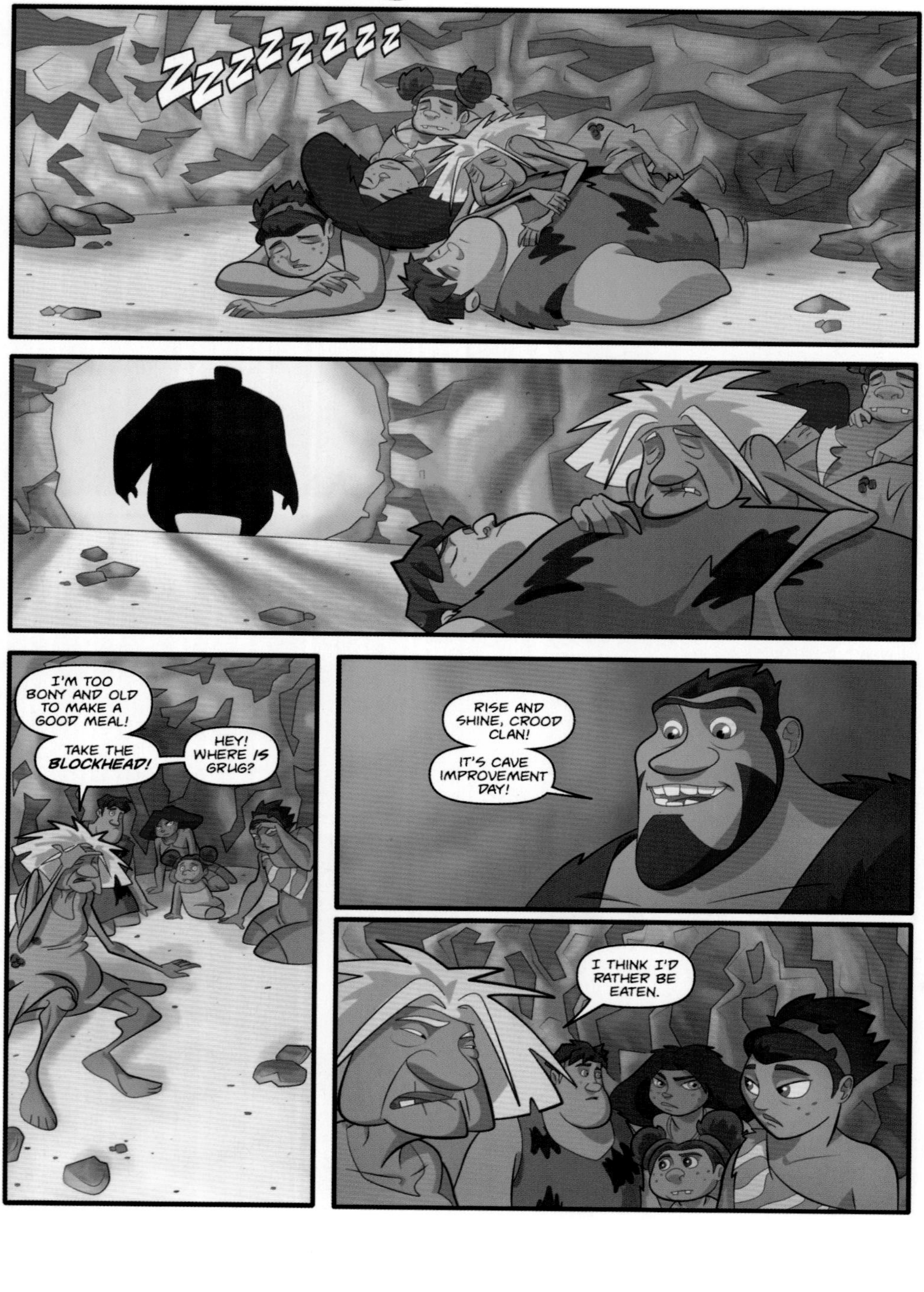
ZZZZZZZZ
I'M TOO BONY AND OLD TO MAKE A GOOD MEAL!
TAKE THE *BLOCKHEAD!*
HEY! WHERE *IS* GRUG?
RISE AND SHINE, CROOD CLAN!
IT'S CAVE IMPROVEMENT DAY!
I THINK I'D RATHER BE EATEN.

The repairs begin...

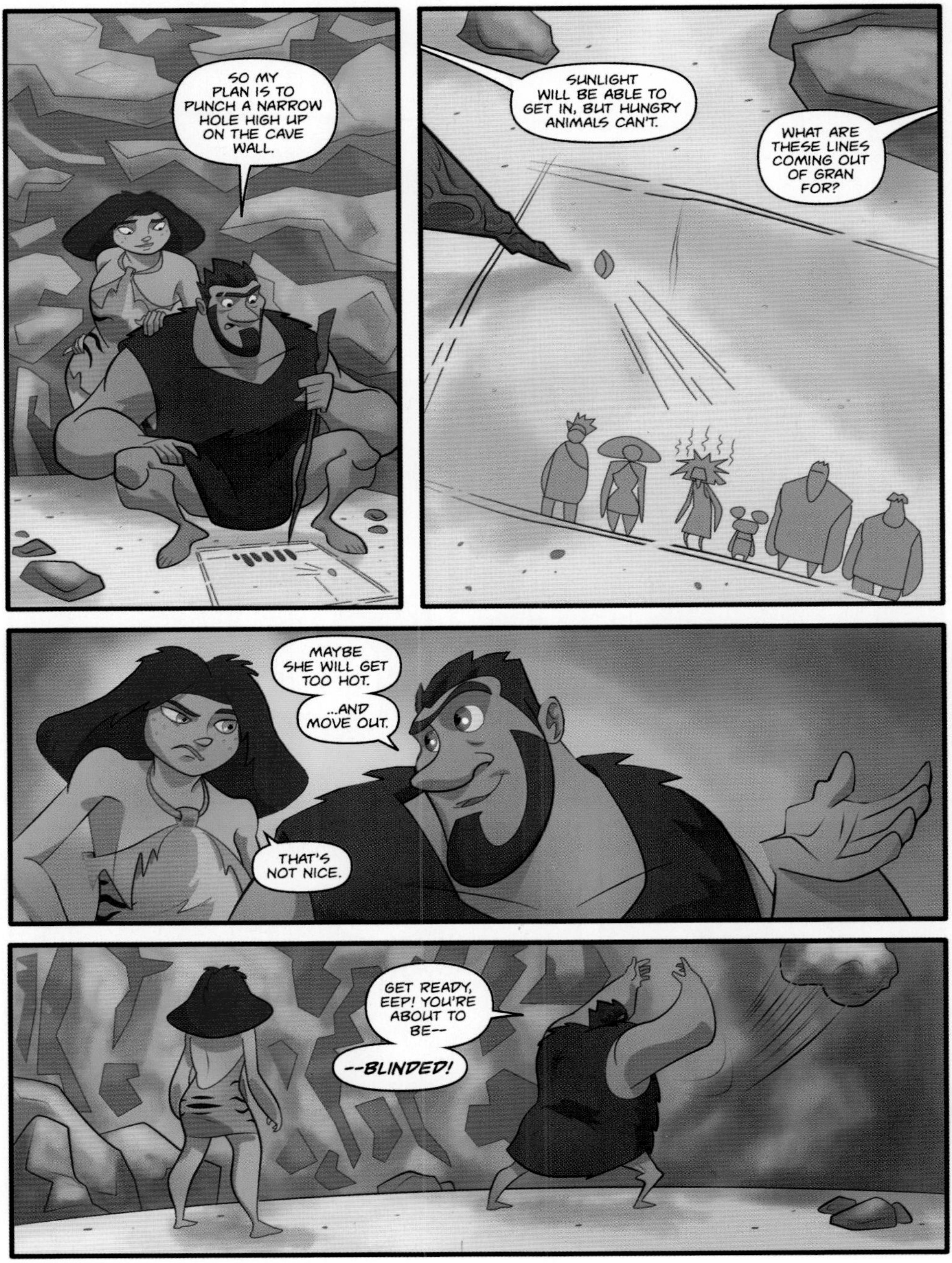

SO MY PLAN IS TO PUNCH A NARROW HOLE HIGH UP ON THE CAVE WALL.
SUNLIGHT WILL BE ABLE TO GET IN, BUT HUNGRY ANIMALS CAN'T.
WHAT ARE THESE LINES COMING OUT OF GRAN FOR?
MAYBE SHE WILL GET TOO HOT.
...AND MOVE OUT.
THAT'S NOT NICE.
GET READY, EEP! YOU'RE ABOUT TO BE--
--BLINDED!

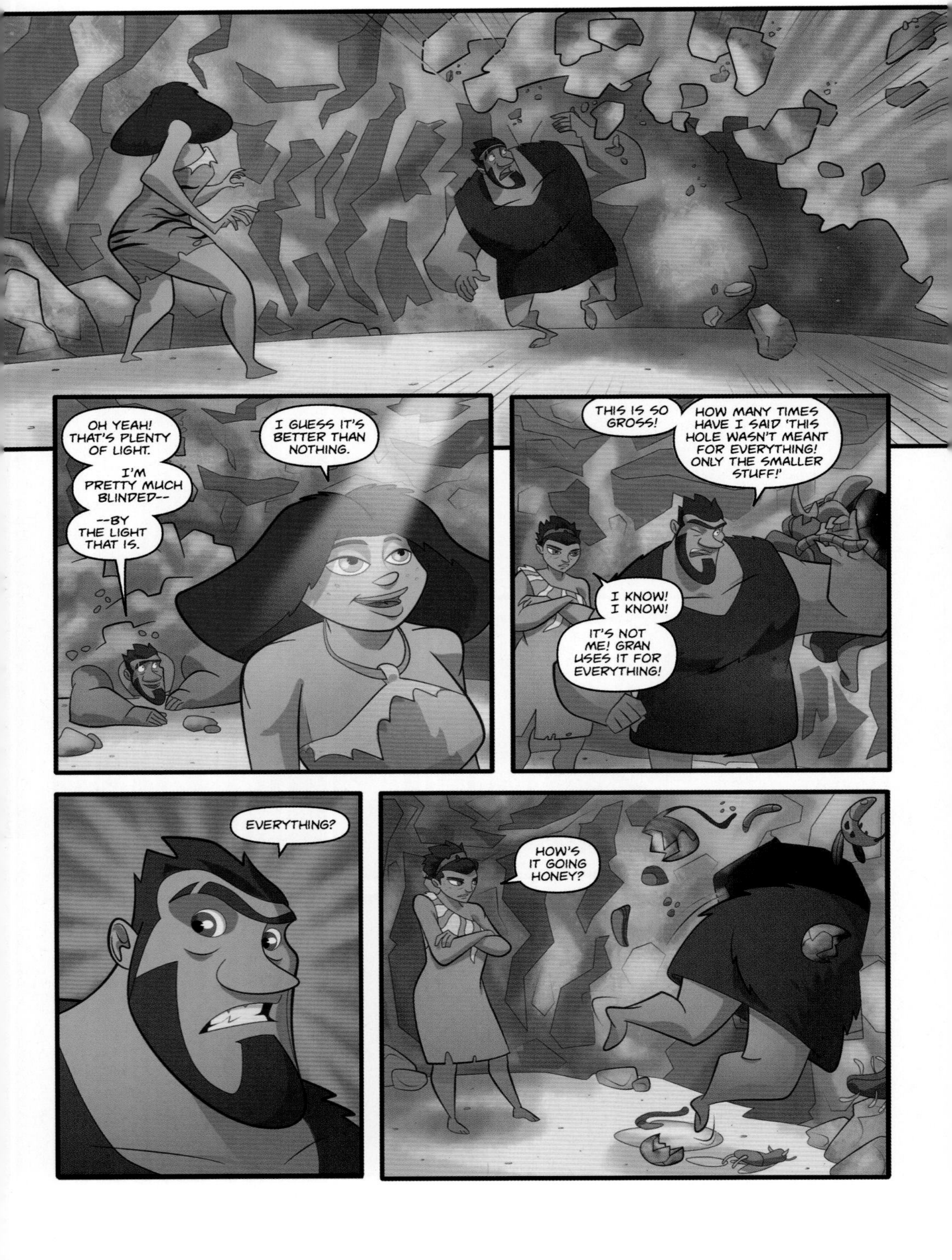
OH YEAH! THAT'S PLENTY OF LIGHT.
I'M PRETTY MUCH BLINDED--
--BY THE LIGHT THAT IS.
I GUESS IT'S BETTER THAN NOTHING.
THIS IS SO GROSS!
HOW MANY TIMES HAVE I SAID 'THIS HOLE WASN'T MEANT FOR EVERYTHING! ONLY THE SMALLER STUFF!'
I KNOW! I KNOW!
IT'S NOT ME! GRAN USES IT FOR EVERYTHING!
EVERYTHING?
HOW'S IT GOING HONEY?

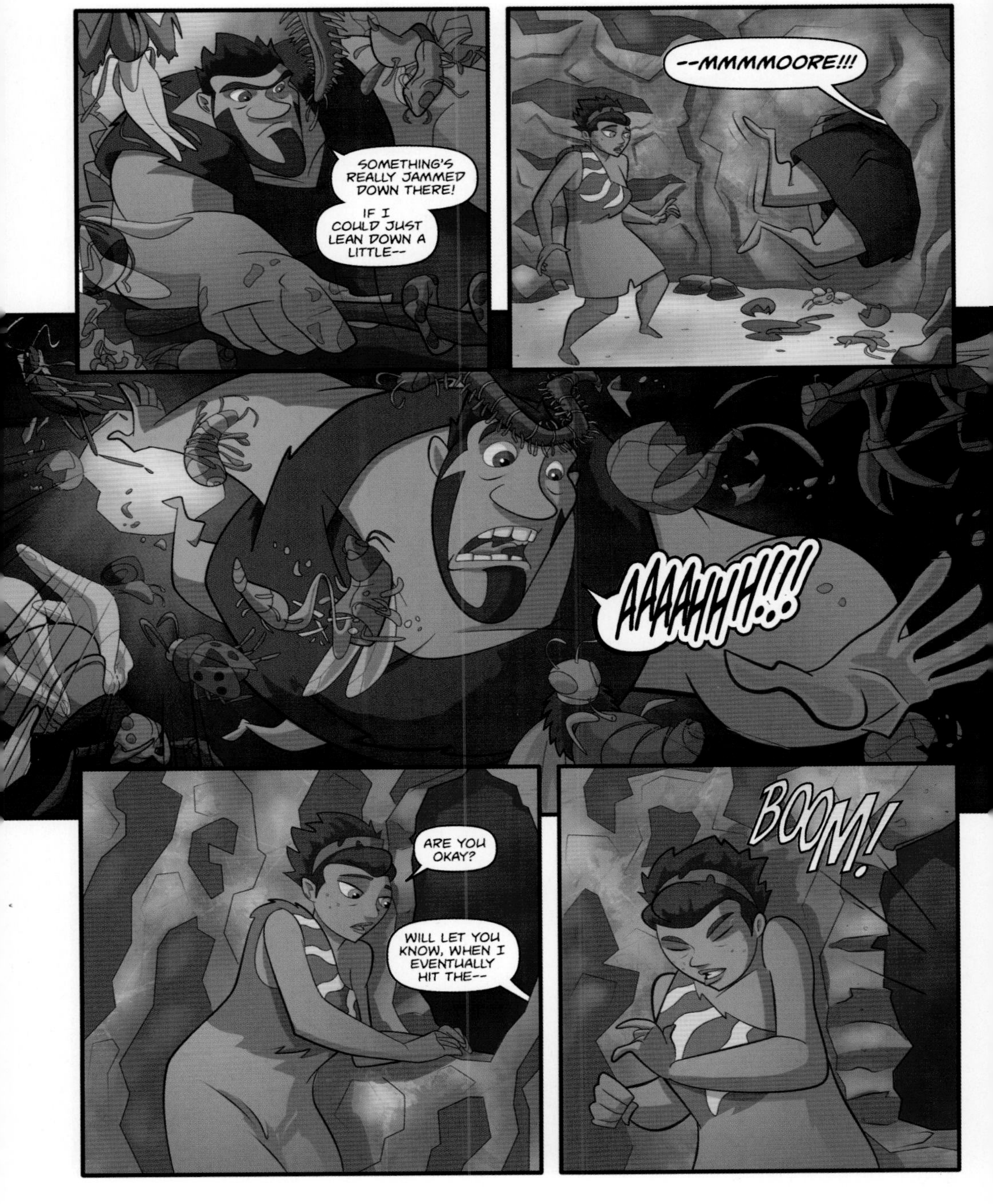
SOMETHING'S REALLY JAMMED DOWN THERE!
IF I COULD JUST LEAN DOWN A LITTLE--
--MMMMOORE!!!
AAAAHHH!!!
ARE YOU OKAY?
WILL LET YOU KNOW, WHEN I EVENTUALLY HIT THE--
BOOM!

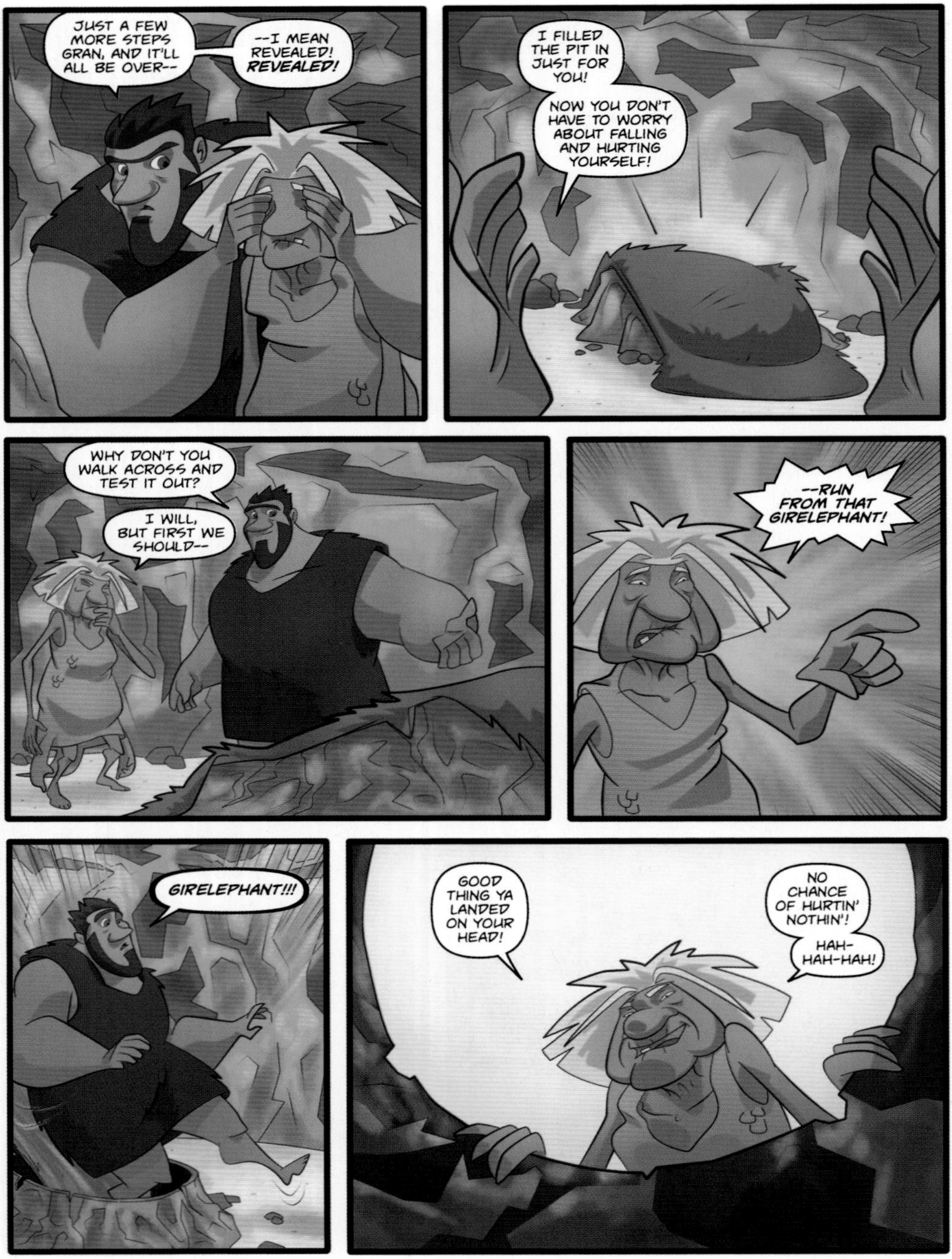
JUST A FEW MORE STEPS GRAN, AND IT'LL ALL BE OVER--
--I MEAN REVEALED! ***REVEALED!***
I FILLED THE PIT IN JUST FOR YOU!
NOW YOU DON'T HAVE TO WORRY ABOUT FALLING AND HURTING YOURSELF!
WHY DON'T YOU WALK ACROSS AND TEST IT OUT?
I WILL, BUT FIRST WE SHOULD--
--RUN FROM THAT GIRELEPHANT!
GIRELEPHANT!!!
GOOD THING YA LANDED ON YOUR HEAD!
NO CHANCE OF HURTIN' NOTHIN'!
HAH-HAH-HAH!

Later that day, after Grug finally climbed out of the pit.

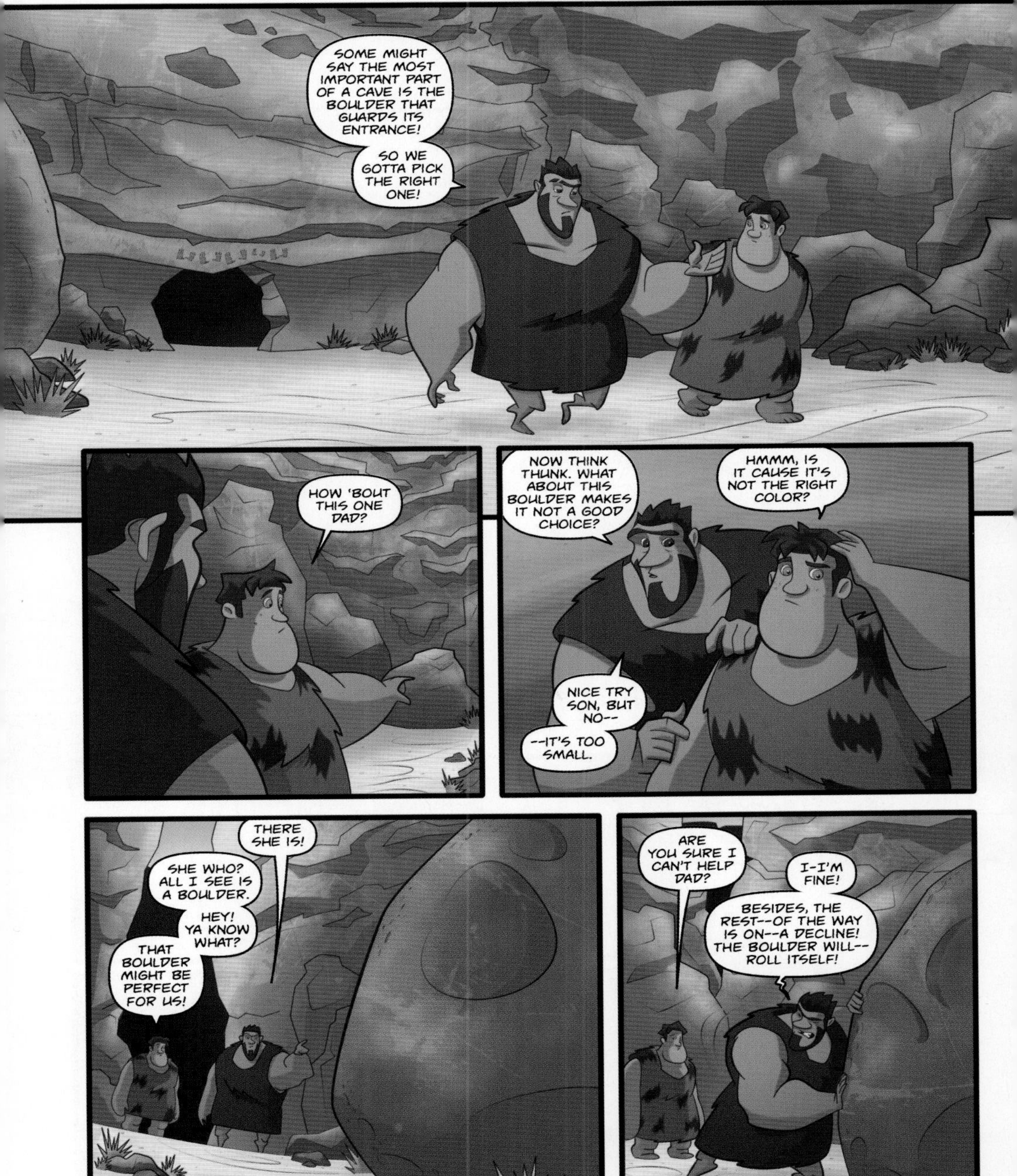
SOME MIGHT SAY THE MOST IMPORTANT PART OF A CAVE IS THE BOULDER THAT GUARDS ITS ENTRANCE!
SO WE GOTTA PICK THE RIGHT ONE!
HOW 'BOUT THIS ONE DAD?
NOW THINK THUNK. WHAT ABOUT THIS BOULDER MAKES IT NOT A GOOD CHOICE?
HMMM, IS IT CAUSE IT'S NOT THE RIGHT COLOR?
NICE TRY SON, BUT NO--
--IT'S TOO SMALL.
THERE SHE IS!
SHE WHO? ALL I SEE IS A BOULDER.
HEY! YA KNOW WHAT?
THAT BOULDER MIGHT BE PERFECT FOR US!
ARE YOU SURE I CAN'T HELP DAD?
I-I'M FINE!
BESIDES, THE REST--OF THE WAY IS ON--A DECLINE! THE BOULDER WILL--ROLL ITSELF!

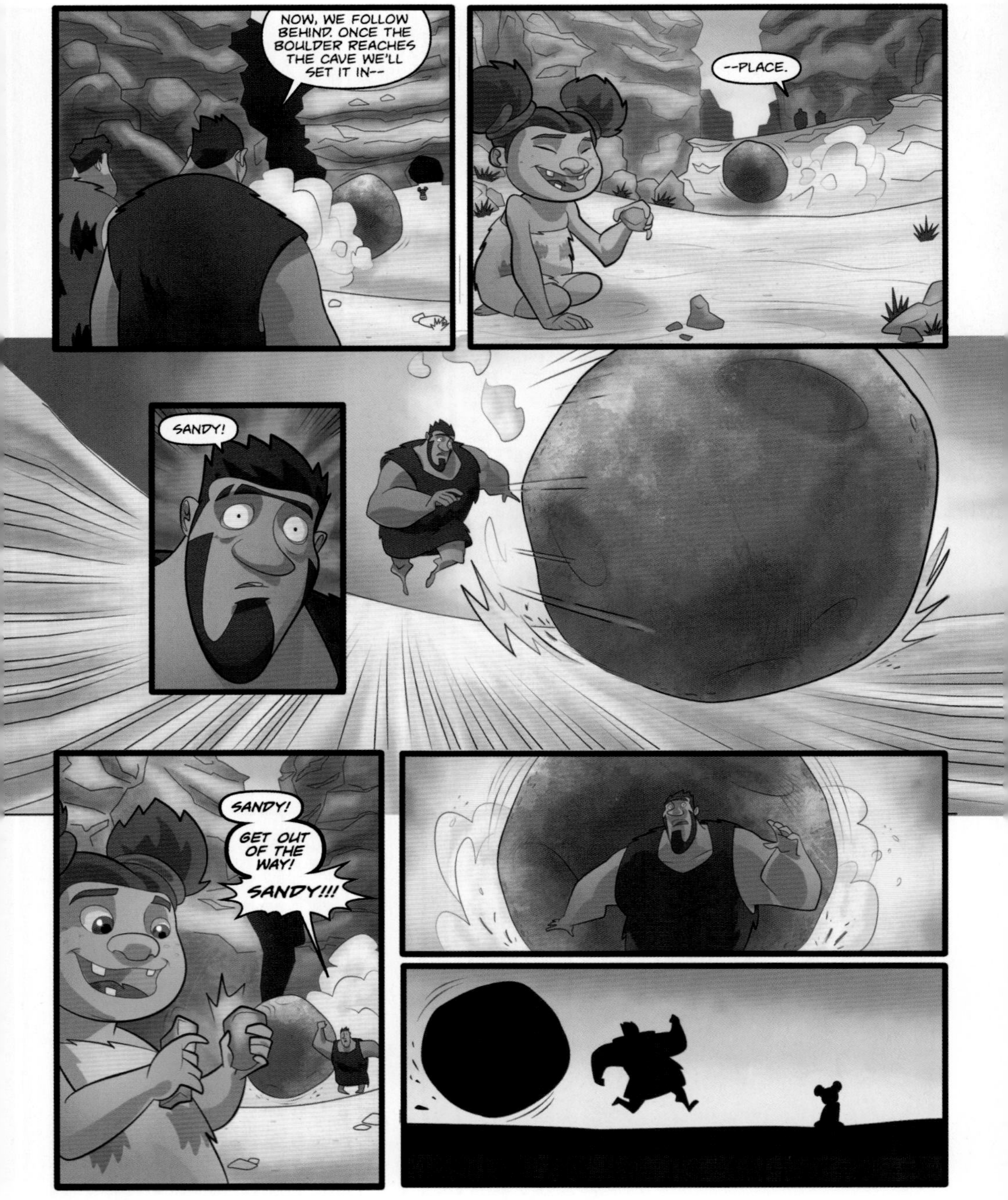
NOW, WE FOLLOW BEHIND. ONCE THE BOULDER REACHES THE CAVE WE'LL SET IT IN--
--PLACE.
SANDY!
SANDY!
GET OUT OF THE WAY!
SANDY!!!

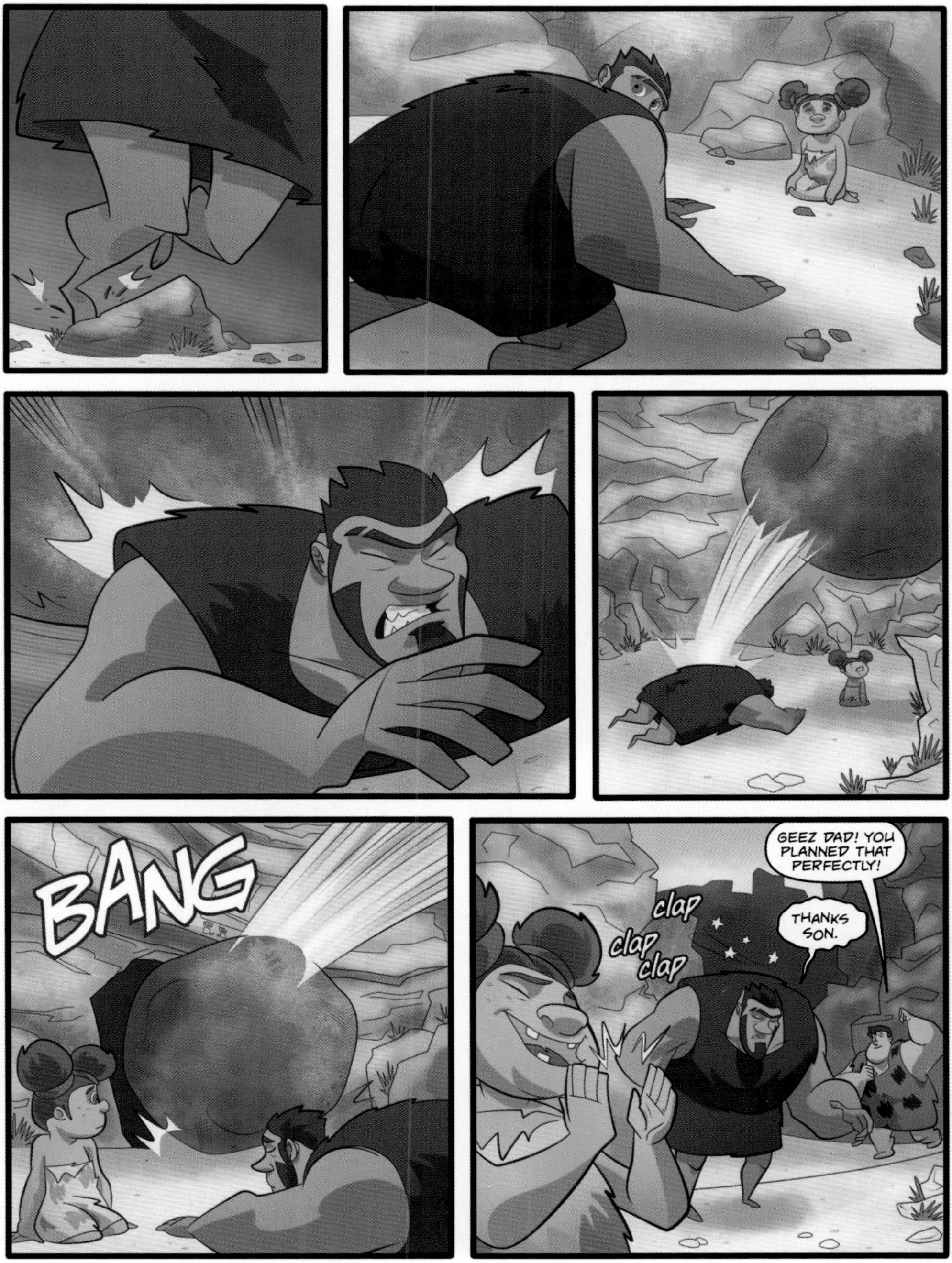
BANG
clap
clap
clap
GEEZ DAD! YOU PLANNED THAT PERFECTLY!
THANKS SON.

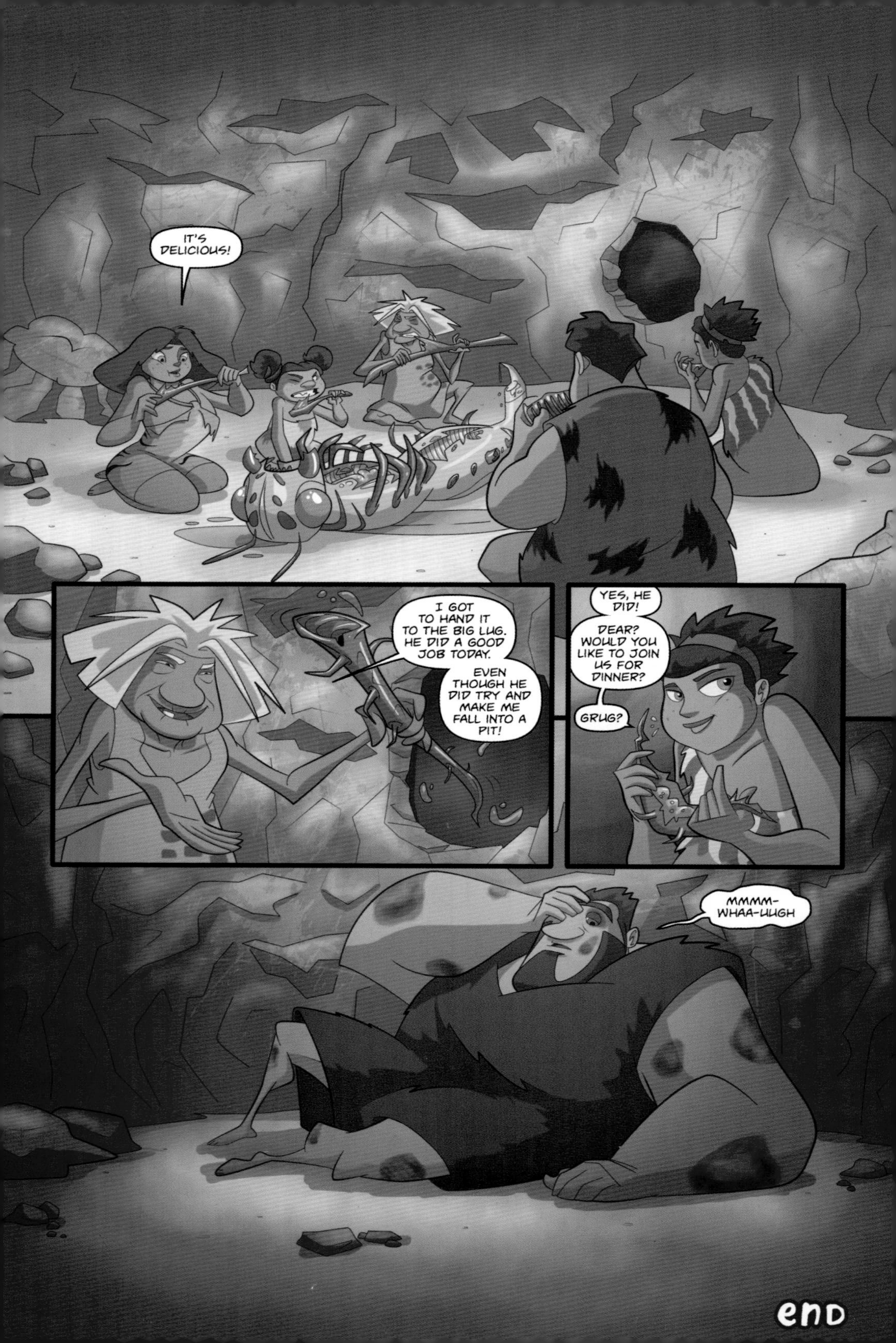
IT'S DELICIOUS!
I GOT TO HAND IT TO THE BIG LUG. HE DID A GOOD JOB TODAY.
EVEN THOUGH HE DID TRY AND MAKE ME FALL INTO A PIT!
YES, HE DID!
DEAR? WOULD YOU LIKE TO JOIN US FOR DINNER?
GRUG?
MMMM-WHAA-UUGH
end

MACAWNIVORE

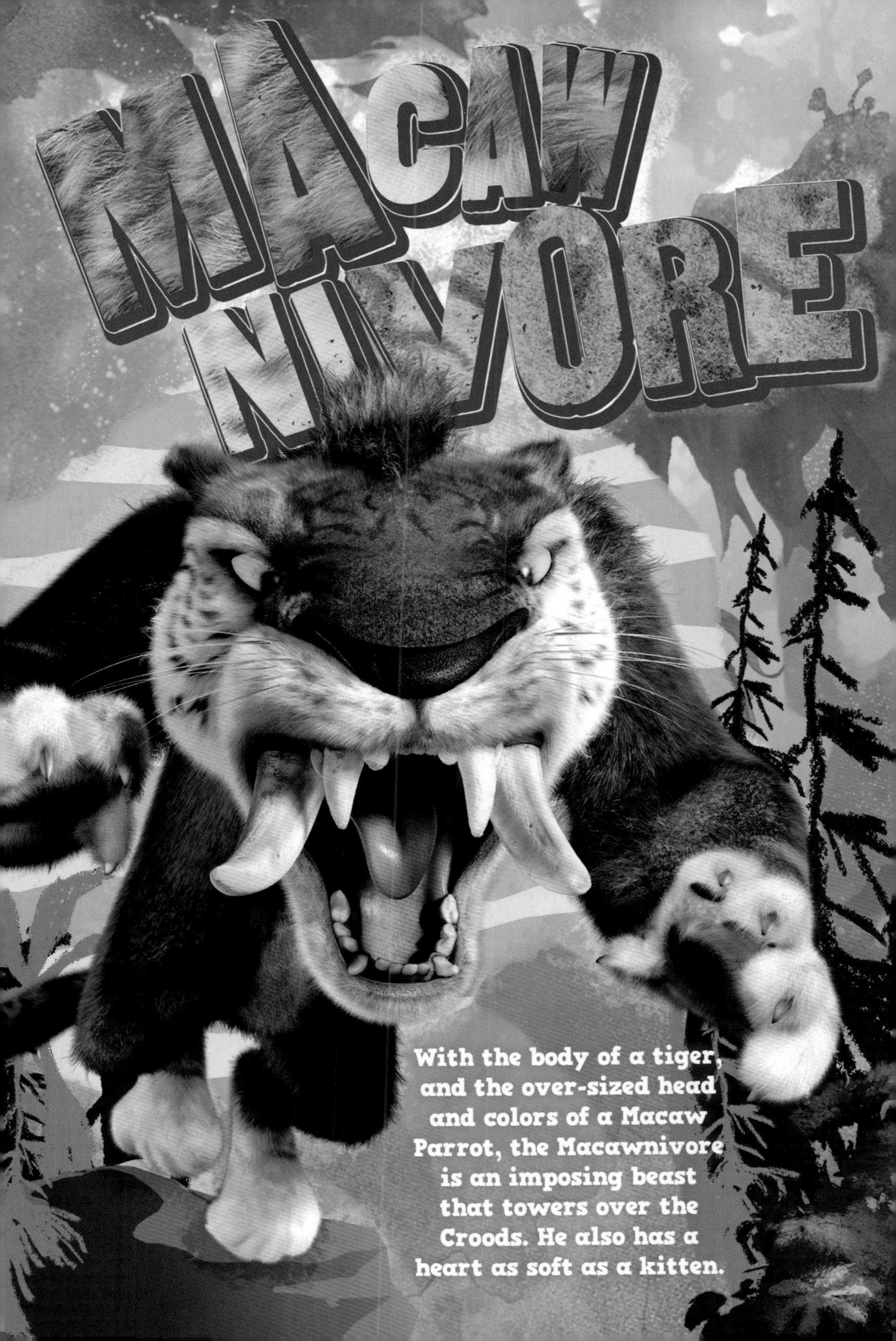

With the body of a tiger, and the over-sized head and colors of a Macaw Parrot, the Macawnivore is an imposing beast that towers over the Croods. He also has a heart as soft as a kitten.

GRUG

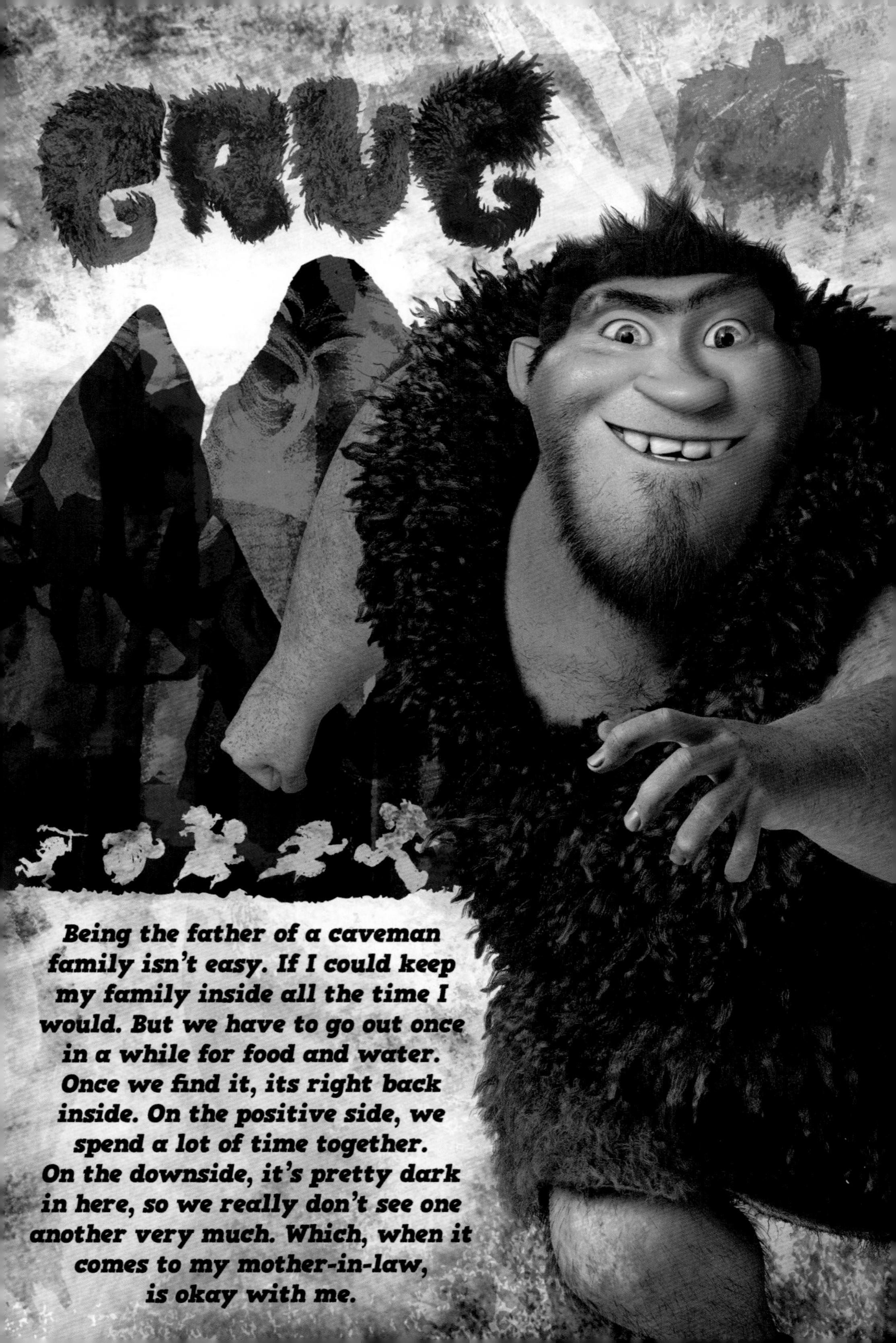

Being the father of a caveman family isn't easy. If I could keep my family inside all the time I would. But we have to go out once in a while for food and water. Once we find it, its right back inside. On the positive side, we spend a lot of time together. On the downside, it's pretty dark in here, so we really don't see one another very much. Which, when it comes to my mother-in-law, is okay with me.

Okay, I know what you're thinking. Living in the Croodaceous period isn't exactly a party. But there's really some nice things about it. Staying in a dark cave is really good for your skin, and we never have to worry about the neighbors being too loud since they were carried away by a dust storm a few summers ago. I do miss sharing mosquito burger recipes with the Throgs, they were nice cave people. But you never know, they might get blown back this way someday.

UGGA

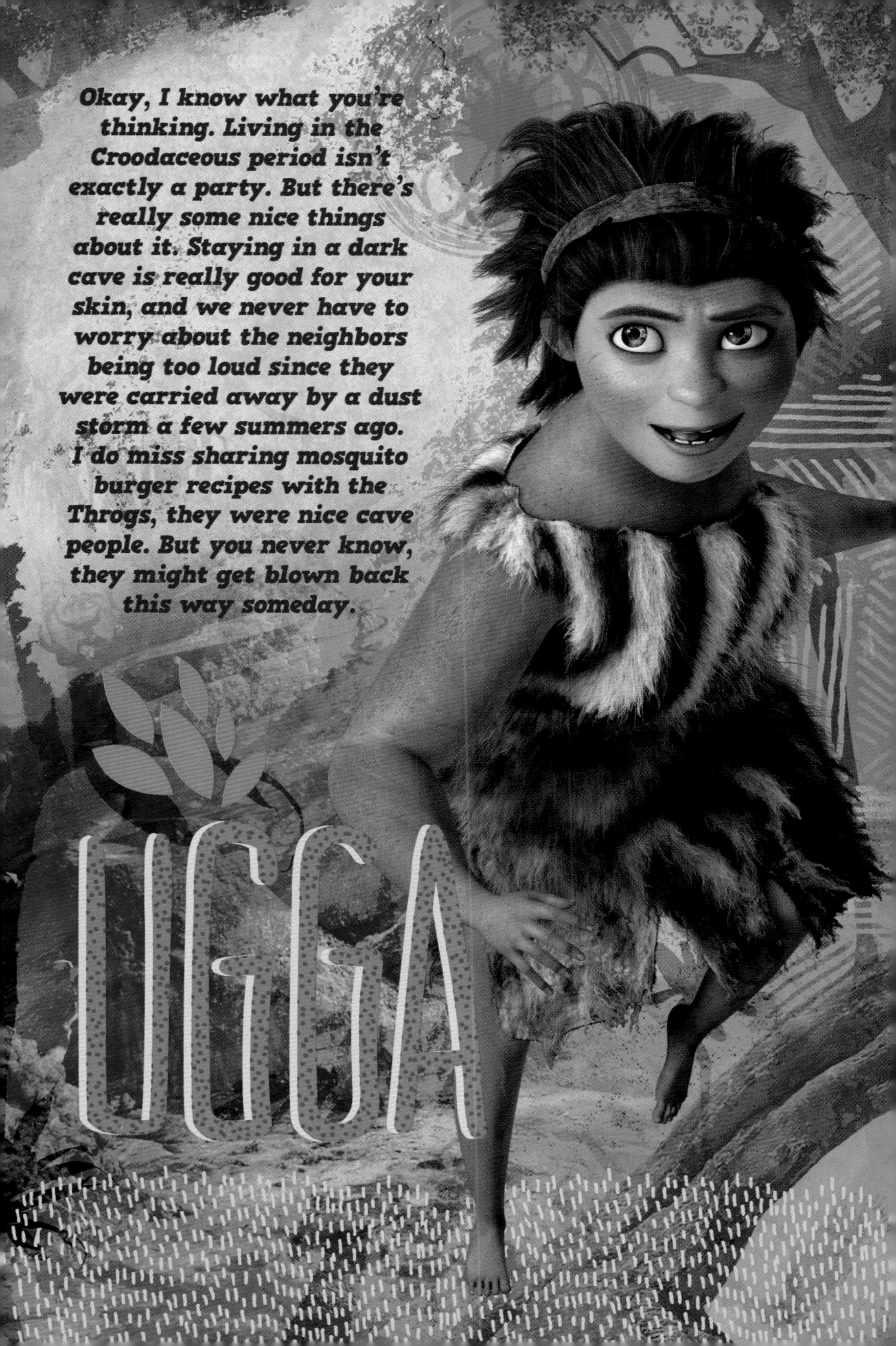

BEAR OWL

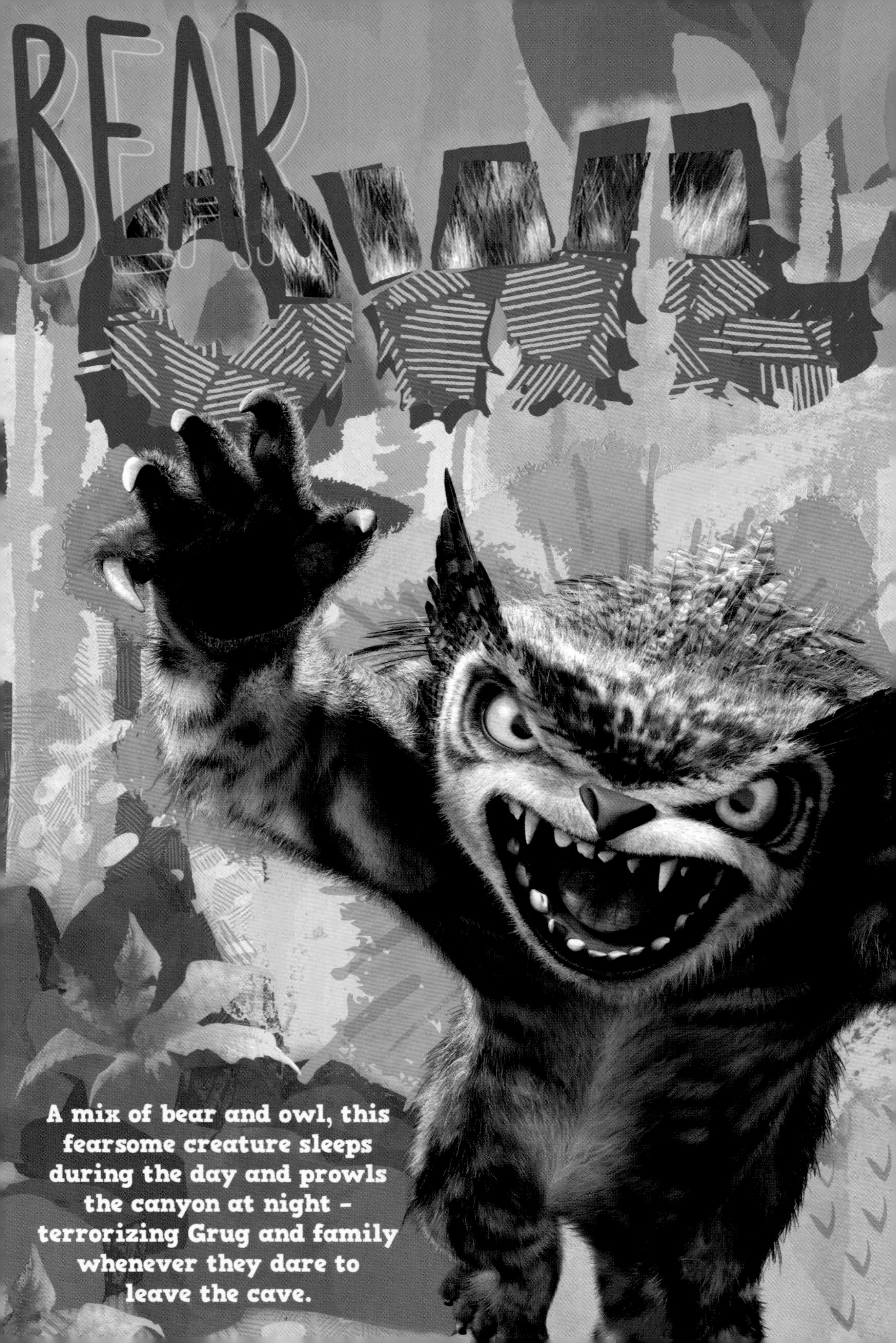

A mix of bear and owl, this fearsome creature sleeps during the day and prowls the canyon at night – terrorizing Grug and family whenever they dare to leave the cave.

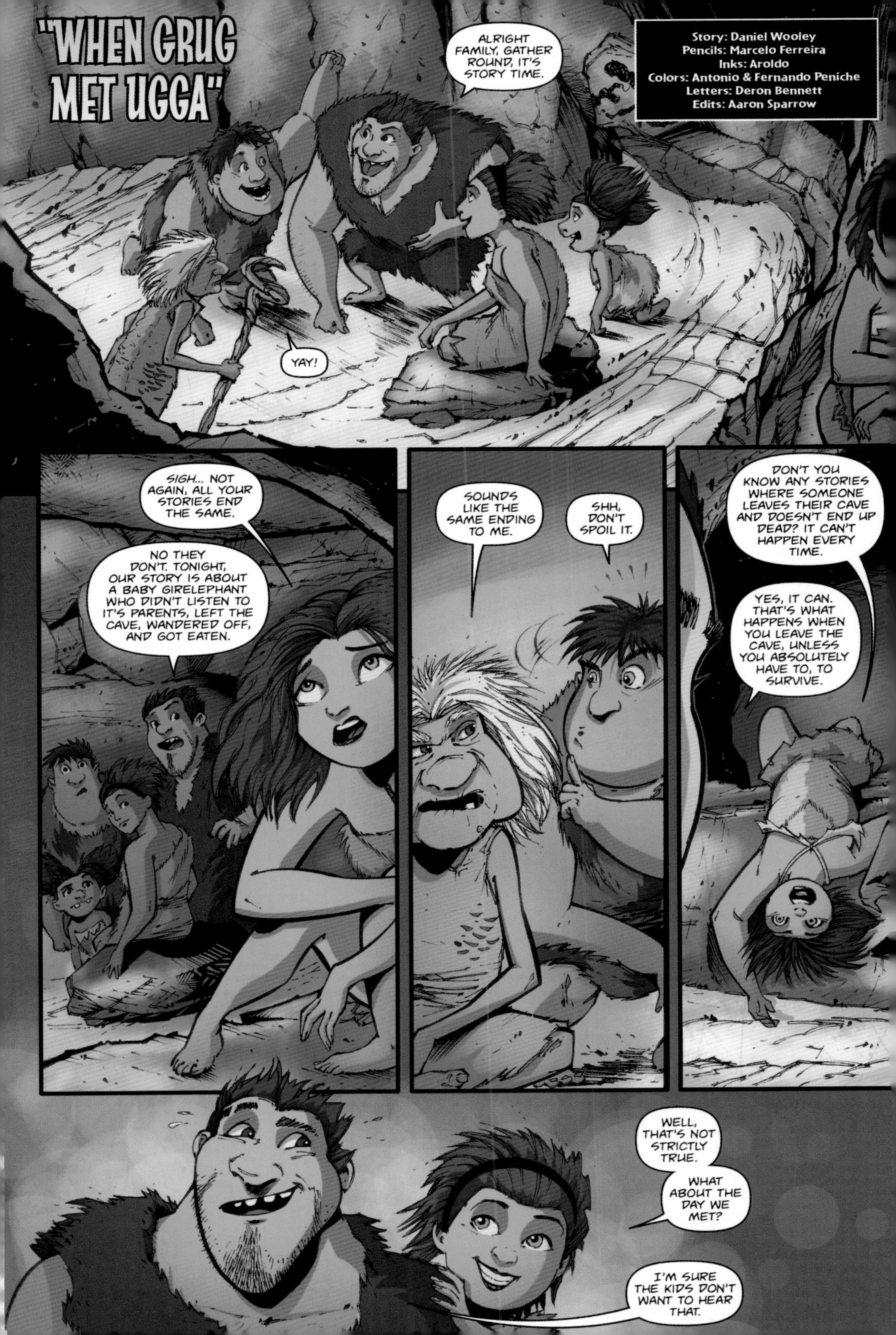

"WHEN GRUG MET UGGA"
Story: Daniel Wooley
Pencils: Marcelo Ferreira
Inks: Aroldo
Colors: Antonio & Fernando Peniche
Letters: Deron Bennett
Edits: Aaron Sparrow
ALRIGHT FAMILY, GATHER ROUND, IT'S STORY TIME.
YAY!
SIGH... NOT AGAIN, ALL YOUR STORIES END THE SAME.
NO THEY DON'T. TONIGHT, OUR STORY IS ABOUT A BABY GIRELEPHANT WHO DIDN'T LISTEN TO IT'S PARENTS, LEFT THE CAVE, WANDERED OFF, AND GOT EATEN.
SOUNDS LIKE THE SAME ENDING TO ME.
SHH, DON'T SPOIL IT.
DON'T YOU KNOW ANY STORIES WHERE SOMEONE LEAVES THEIR CAVE AND DOESN'T END UP DEAD? IT CAN'T HAPPEN EVERY TIME.
YES, IT CAN. THAT'S WHAT HAPPENS WHEN YOU LEAVE THE CAVE, UNLESS YOU ABSOLUTELY HAVE TO, TO SURVIVE.
WELL, THAT'S NOT STRICTLY TRUE.
WHAT ABOUT THE DAY WE MET?
I'M SURE THE KIDS DON'T WANT TO HEAR THAT.

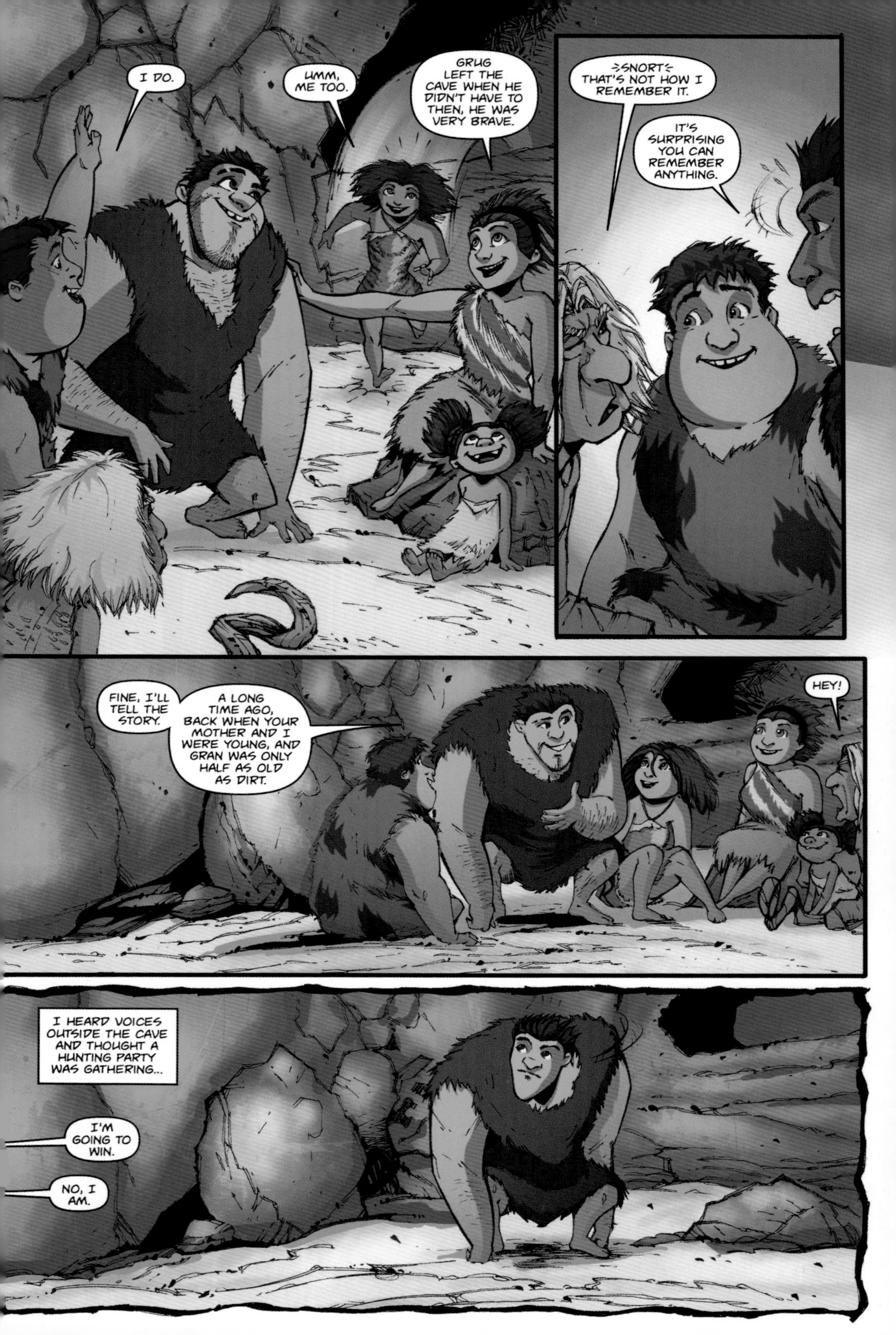
I DO.
UMM, ME TOO.
GRUG LEFT THE CAVE WHEN HE DIDN'T HAVE TO THEN, HE WAS VERY BRAVE.
-SNORT- THAT'S NOT HOW I REMEMBER IT.
IT'S SURPRISING YOU CAN REMEMBER ANYTHING.
FINE, I'LL TELL THE STORY.
A LONG TIME AGO, BACK WHEN YOUR MOTHER AND I WERE YOUNG, AND GRAN WAS ONLY HALF AS OLD AS DIRT.
HEY!
I HEARD VOICES OUTSIDE THE CAVE AND THOUGHT A HUNTING PARTY WAS GATHERING...
I'M GOING TO WIN.
NO, I AM.

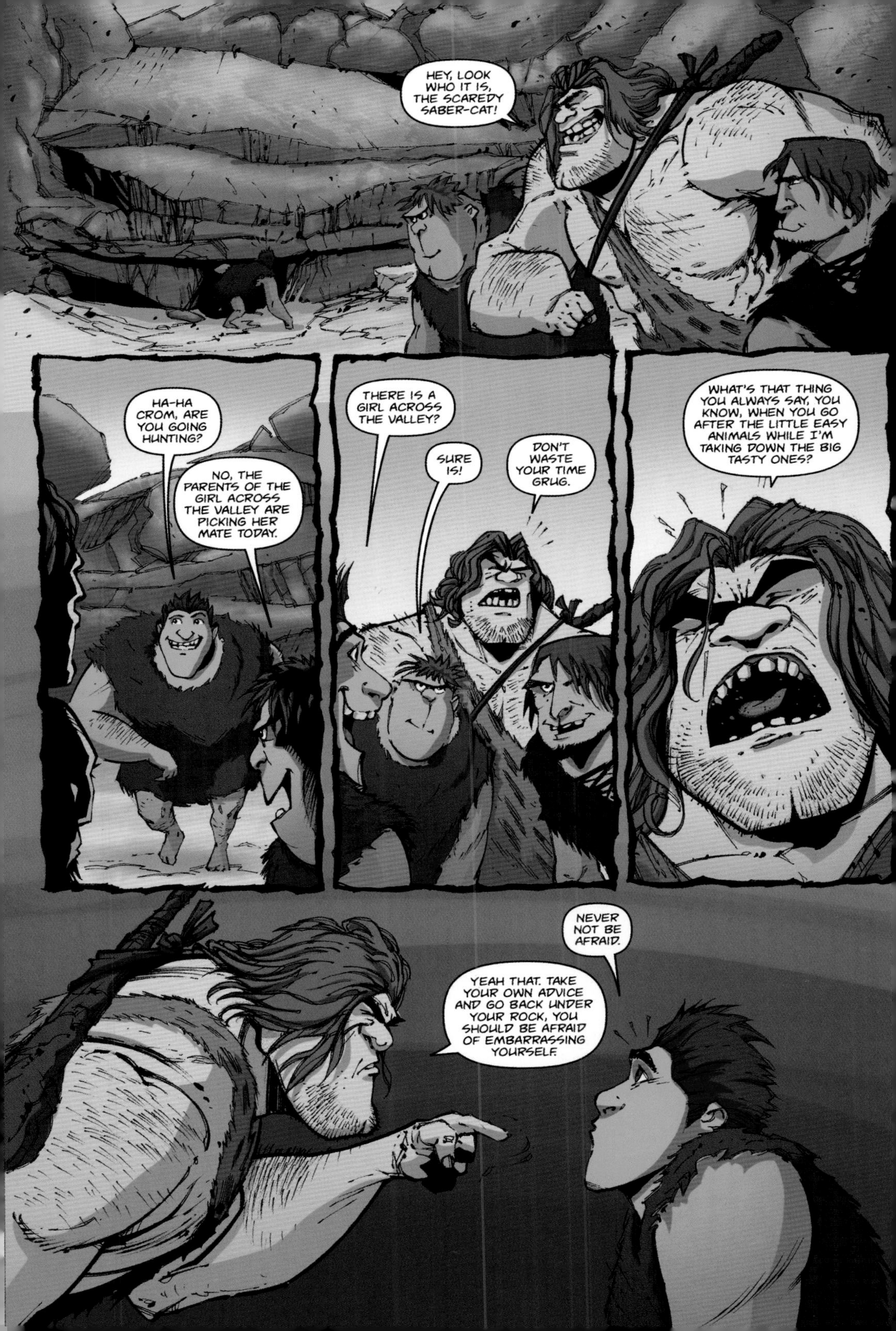
HEY, LOOK WHO IT IS, THE SCAREDY SABER-CAT!
HA-HA CROM, ARE YOU GOING HUNTING?
NO, THE PARENTS OF THE GIRL ACROSS THE VALLEY ARE PICKING HER MATE TODAY.
THERE IS A GIRL ACROSS THE VALLEY?
SURE IS!
DON'T WASTE YOUR TIME GRUG.
WHAT'S THAT THING YOU ALWAYS SAY, YOU KNOW, WHEN YOU GO AFTER THE LITTLE EASY ANIMALS WHILE I'M TAKING DOWN THE BIG TASTY ONES?
NEVER NOT BE AFRAID.
YEAH THAT. TAKE YOUR OWN ADVICE AND GO BACK UNDER YOUR ROCK, YOU SHOULD BE AFRAID OF EMBARRASSING YOURSELF.

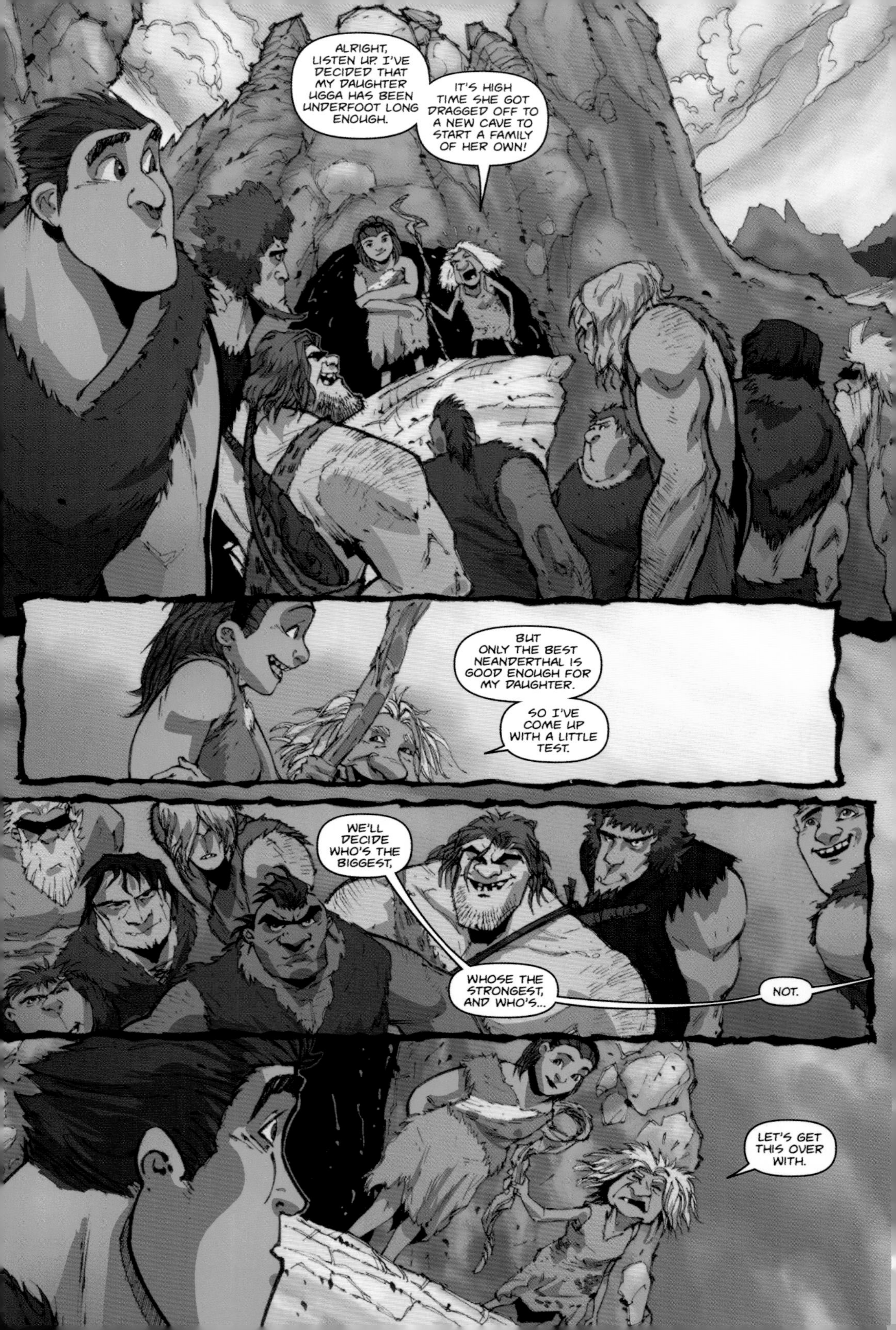

ALRIGHT, LISTEN UP. I'VE DECIDED THAT MY DAUGHTER UGGA HAS BEEN UNDERFOOT LONG ENOUGH.
IT'S HIGH TIME SHE GOT DRAGGED OFF TO A NEW CAVE TO START A FAMILY OF HER OWN!
BUT ONLY THE BEST NEANDERTHAL IS GOOD ENOUGH FOR MY DAUGHTER.
SO I'VE COME UP WITH A LITTLE TEST.
WE'LL DECIDE WHO'S THE BIGGEST,
WHOSE THE STRONGEST, AND WHO'S...
NOT.
LET'S GET THIS OVER WITH.

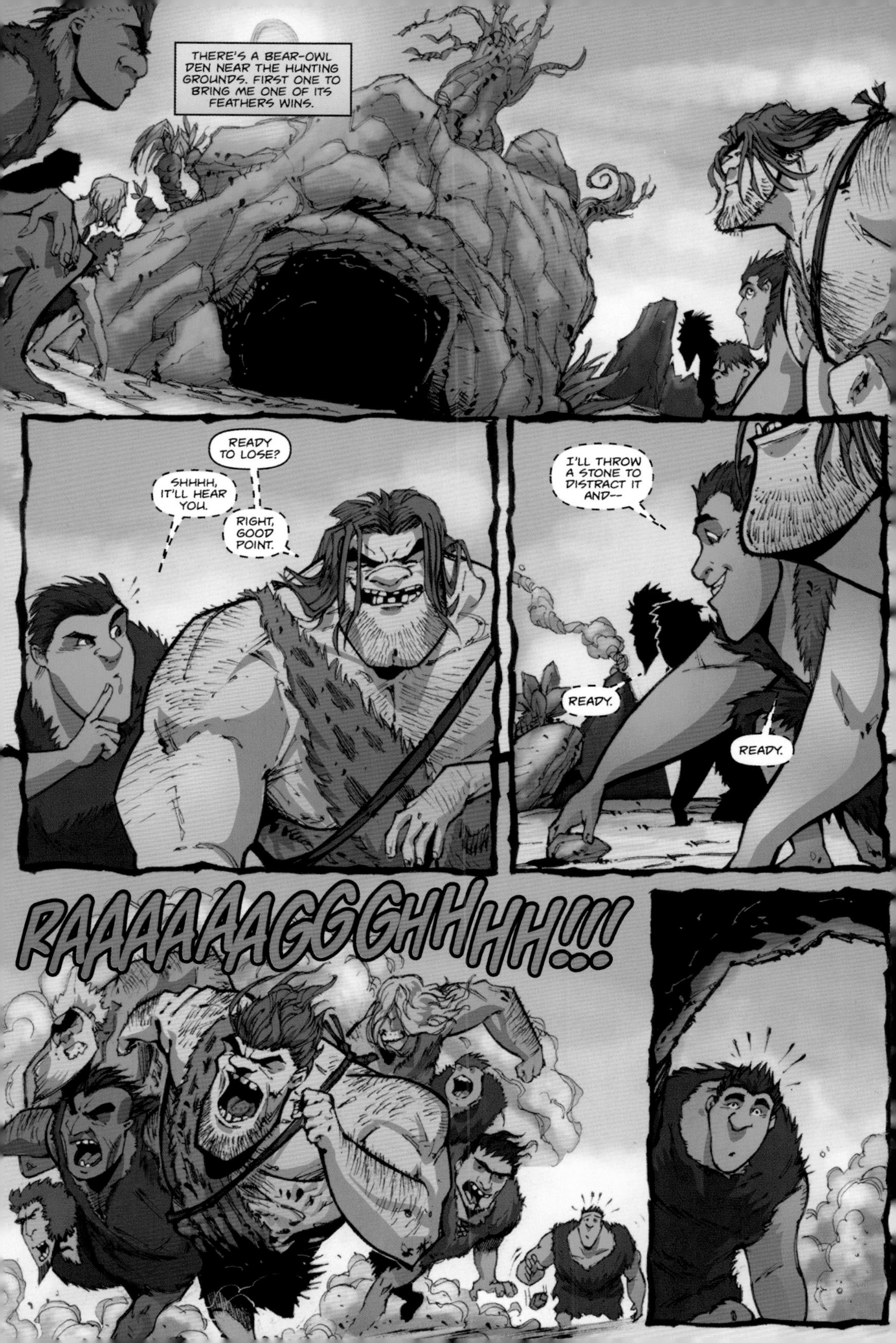
THERE'S A BEAR-OWL DEN NEAR THE HUNTING GROUNDS. FIRST ONE TO BRING ME ONE OF ITS FEATHERS WINS.
READY TO LOSE?
SHHHH, IT'LL HEAR YOU.
RIGHT, GOOD POINT.
I'LL THROW A STONE TO DISTRACT IT AND--
READY.
READY.
RAAAAAAGGGGHHHHH!!!

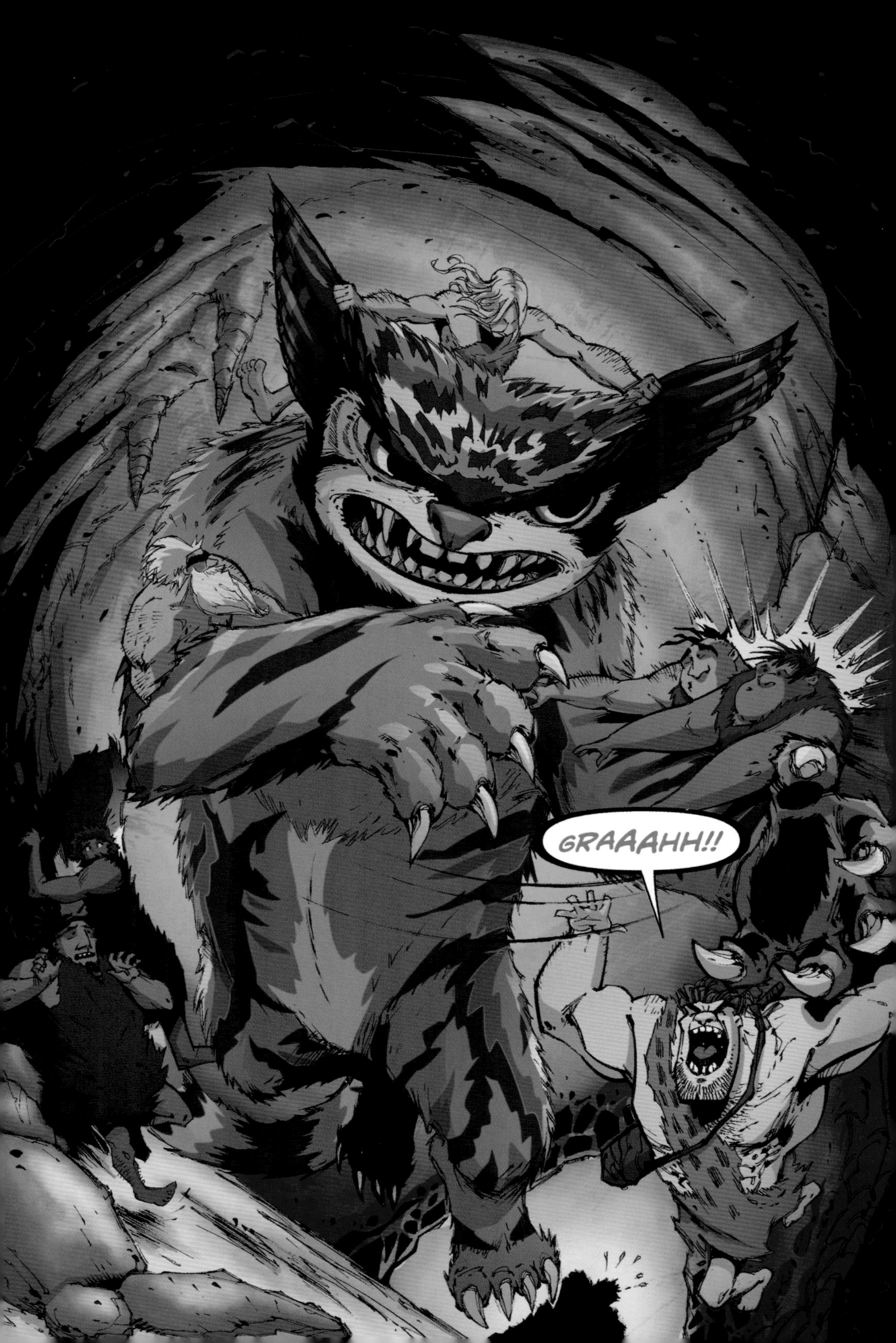
GRAAAHH!!

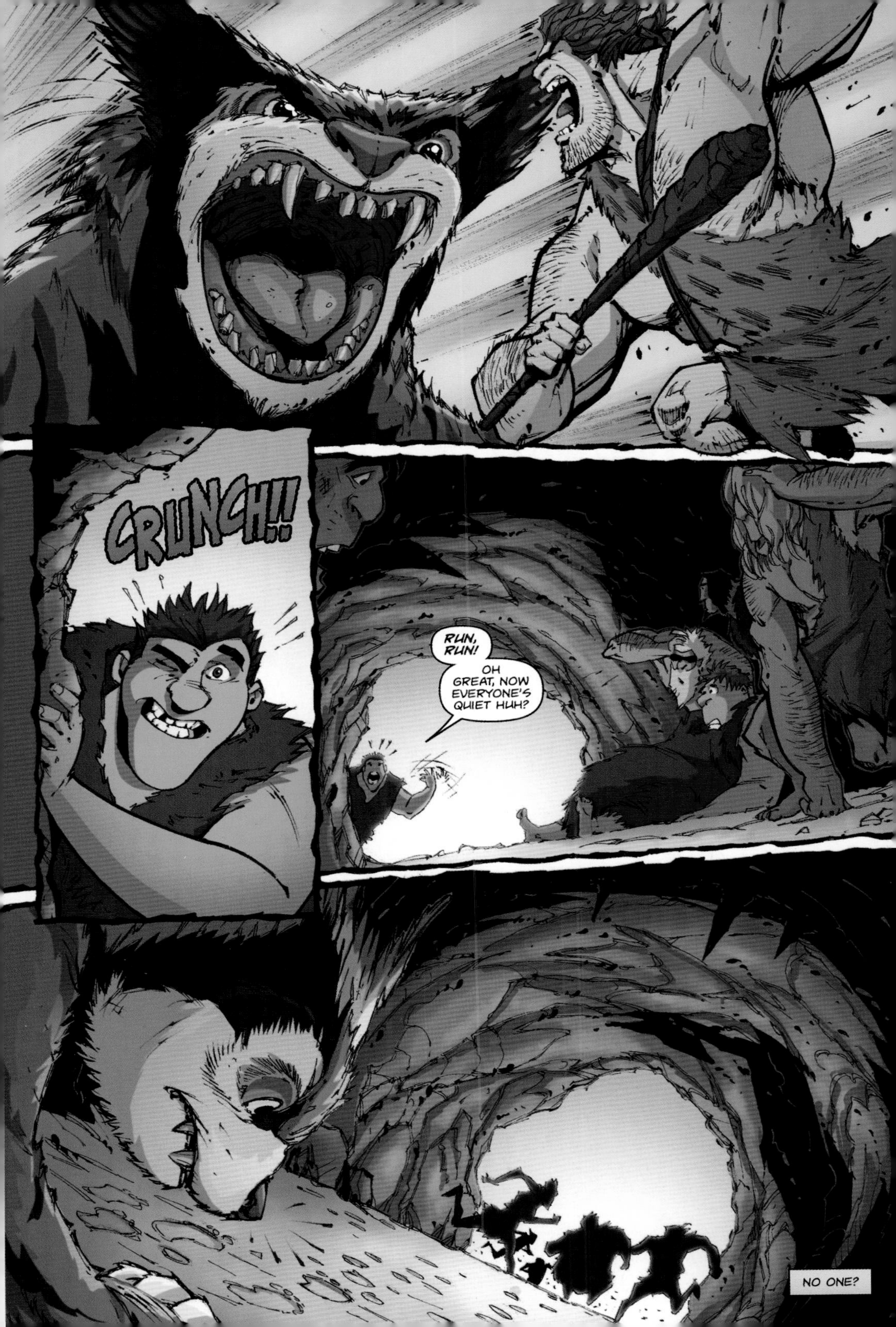
CRUNCH!!
RUN, RUN!
OH GREAT, NOW EVERYONE'S QUIET HUH?
NO ONE?

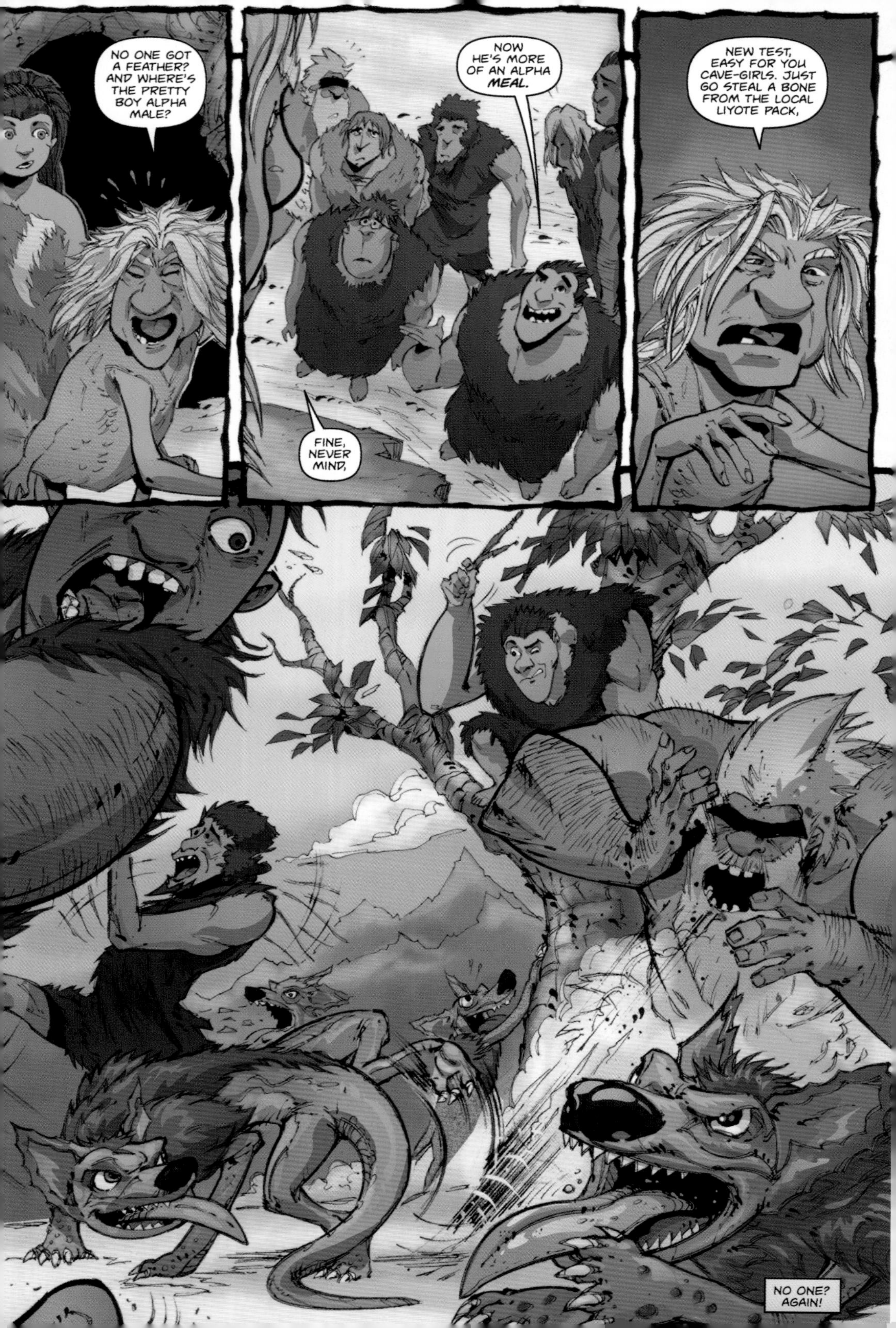

NO ONE GOT A FEATHER? AND WHERE'S THE PRETTY BOY ALPHA MALE?
NOW HE'S MORE OF AN ALPHA MEAL.
FINE, NEVER MIND.
NEW TEST. EASY FOR YOU CAVE-GIRLS. JUST GO STEAL A BONE FROM THE LOCAL LIYOTE PACK.
NO ONE? AGAIN!

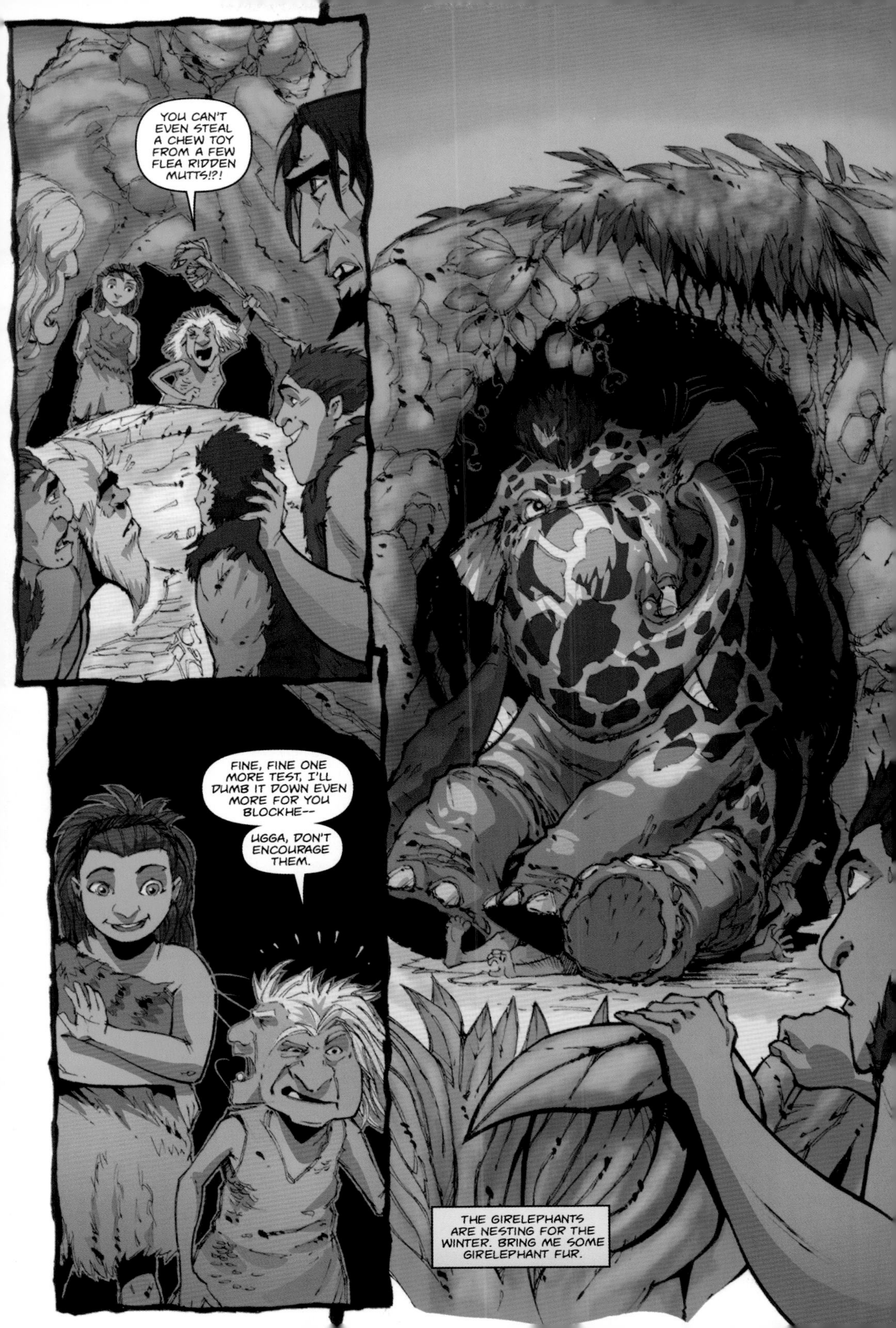
YOU CAN'T EVEN STEAL A CHEW TOY FROM A FEW FLEA RIDDEN MUTTS!?!
FINE, FINE ONE MORE TEST, I'LL DUMB IT DOWN EVEN MORE FOR YOU BLOCKHE--
UGGA, DON'T ENCOURAGE THEM.
THE GIRELEPHANTS ARE NESTING FOR THE WINTER. BRING ME SOME GIRELEPHANT FUR.

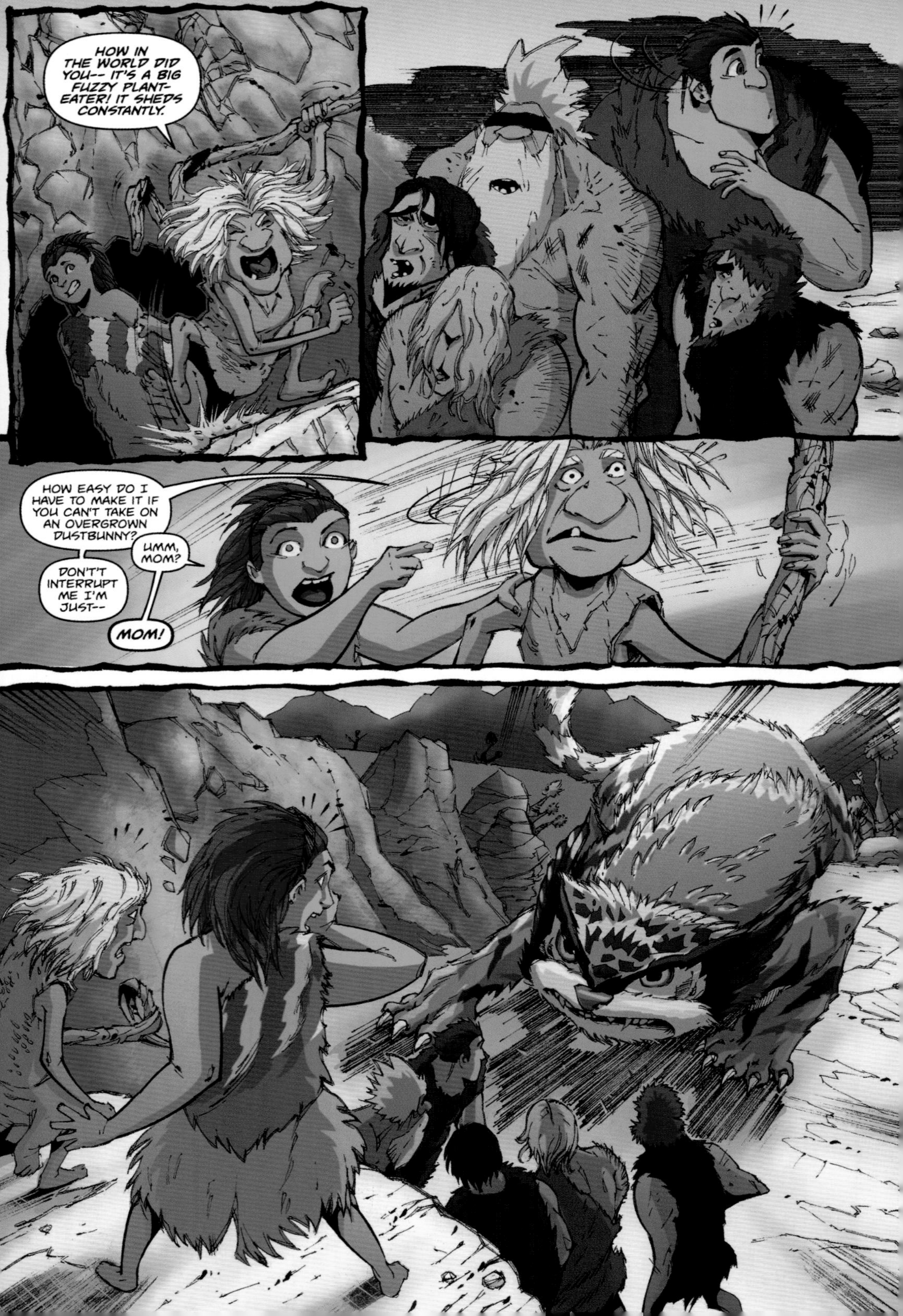

HOW IN THE WORLD DID YOU-- IT'S A BIG FUZZY PLANT-EATER! IT SHEDS CONSTANTLY.
HOW EASY DO I HAVE TO MAKE IT IF YOU CAN'T TAKE ON AN OVERGROWN DUSTBUNNY?
UMM, MOM?
DON'T'T INTERRUPT ME I'M JUST--
MOM!

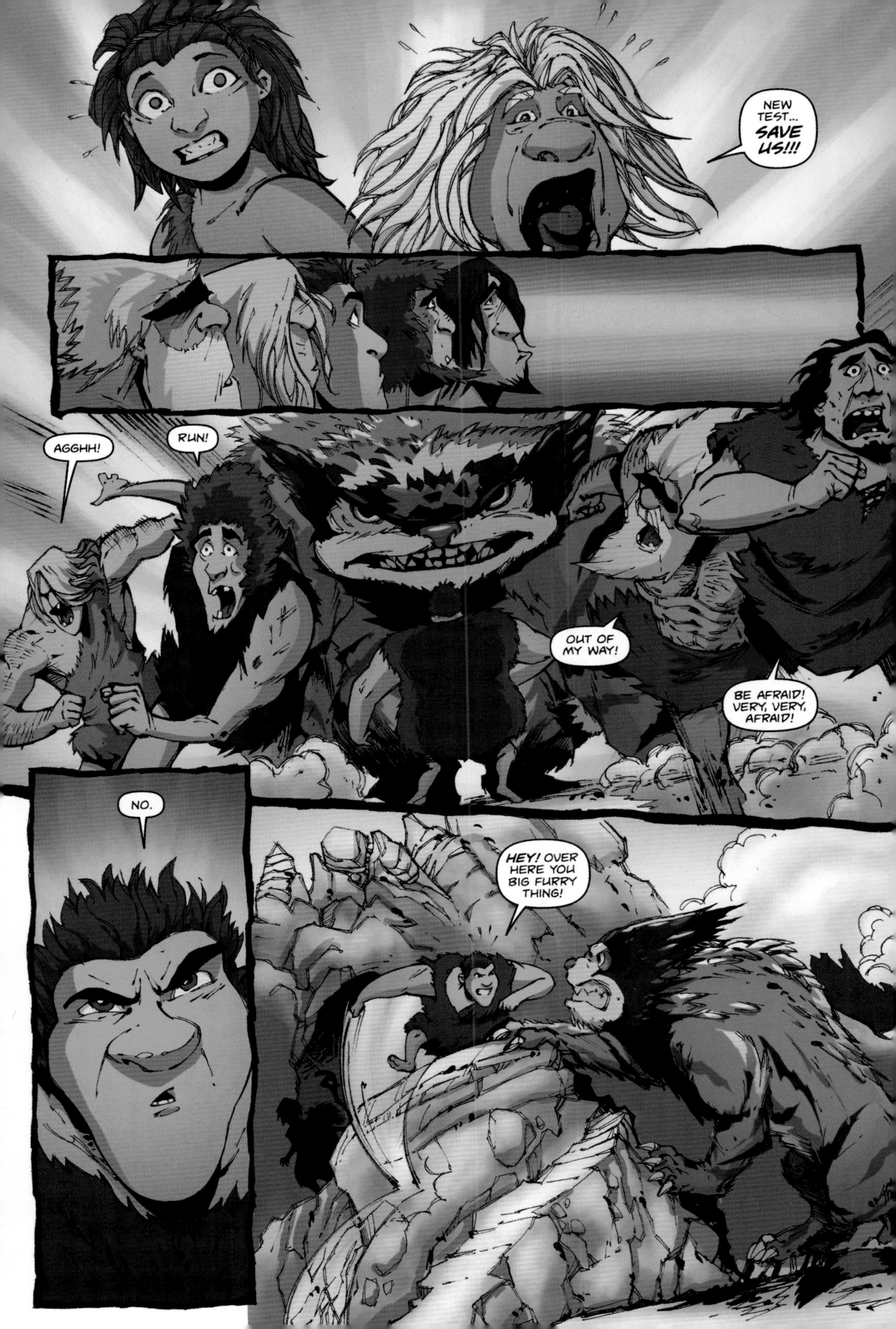
NEW TEST... SAVE US!!!
AGGHH!
RUN!
OUT OF MY WAY!
BE AFRAID! VERY, VERY, AFRAID!
NO.
HEY! OVER HERE YOU BIG FURRY THING!

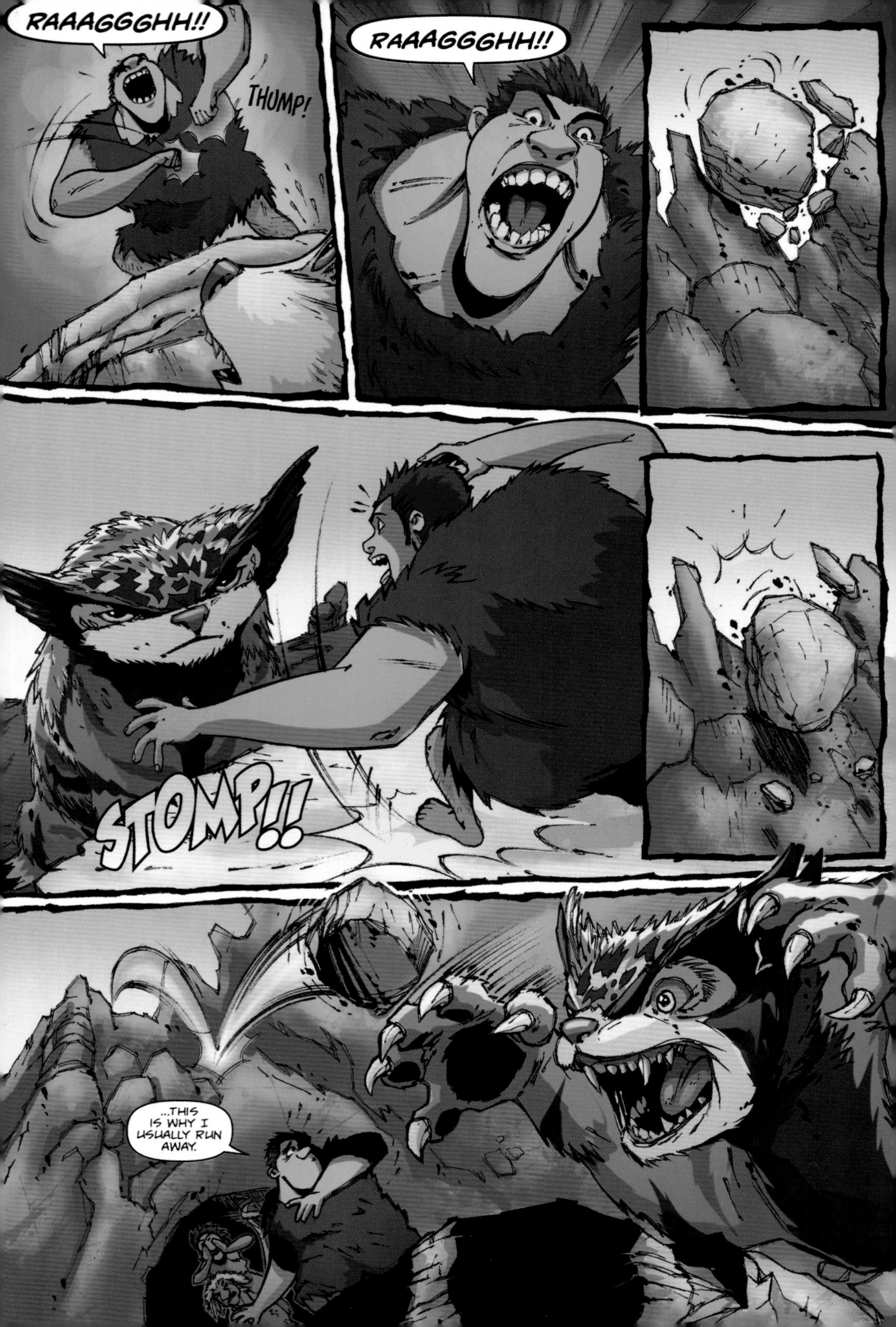
RAAAGGGHH!!
THUMP!
RAAAGGGHH!!
STOMP!!
...THIS IS WHY I USUALLY RUN AWAY.

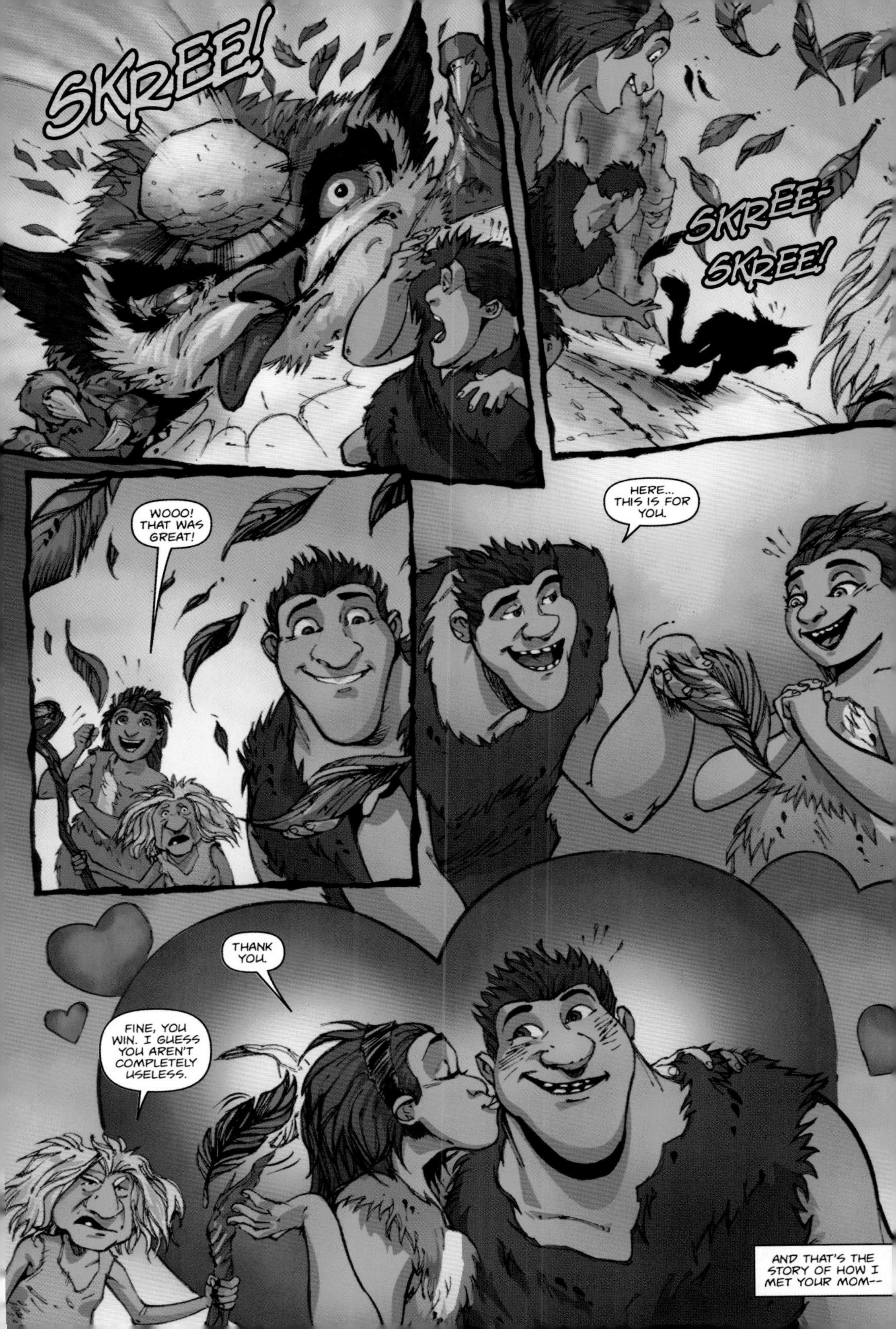
SKREE!
SKREE-SKREE!
WOOO! THAT WAS GREAT!
HERE... THIS IS FOR YOU.
THANK YOU.
FINE, YOU WIN. I GUESS YOU AREN'T COMPLETELY USELESS.
AND THAT'S THE STORY OF HOW I MET YOUR MOM--

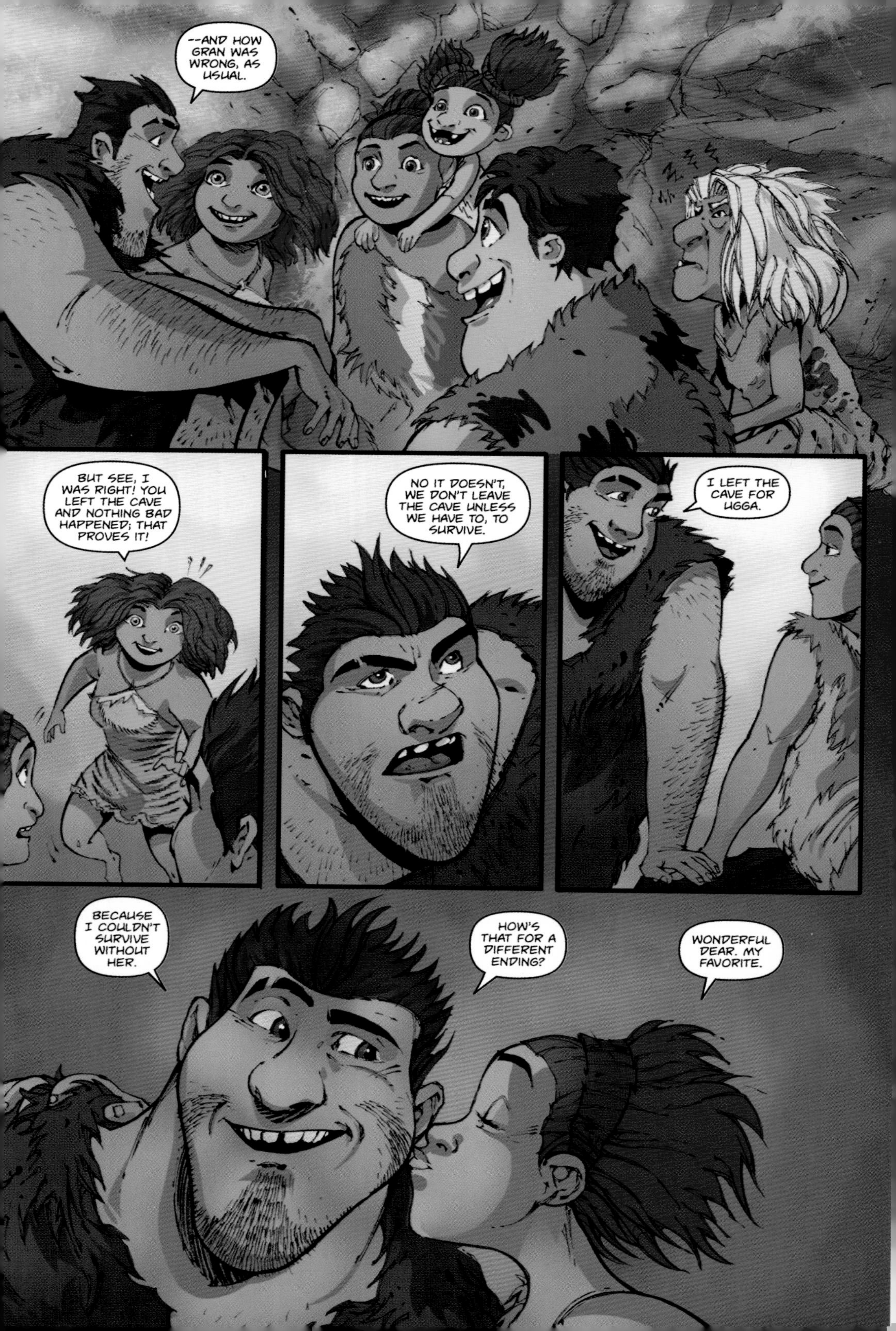
--AND HOW GRAN WAS WRONG, AS USUAL.
BUT SEE, I WAS RIGHT! YOU LEFT THE CAVE AND NOTHING BAD HAPPENED; THAT PROVES IT!
NO IT DOESN'T, WE DON'T LEAVE THE CAVE UNLESS WE HAVE TO, TO SURVIVE.
I LEFT THE CAVE FOR UGGA.
BECAUSE I COULDN'T SURVIVE WITHOUT HER.
HOW'S THAT FOR A DIFFERENT ENDING?
WONDERFUL DEAR. MY FAVORITE.

PUNCH MONKEY

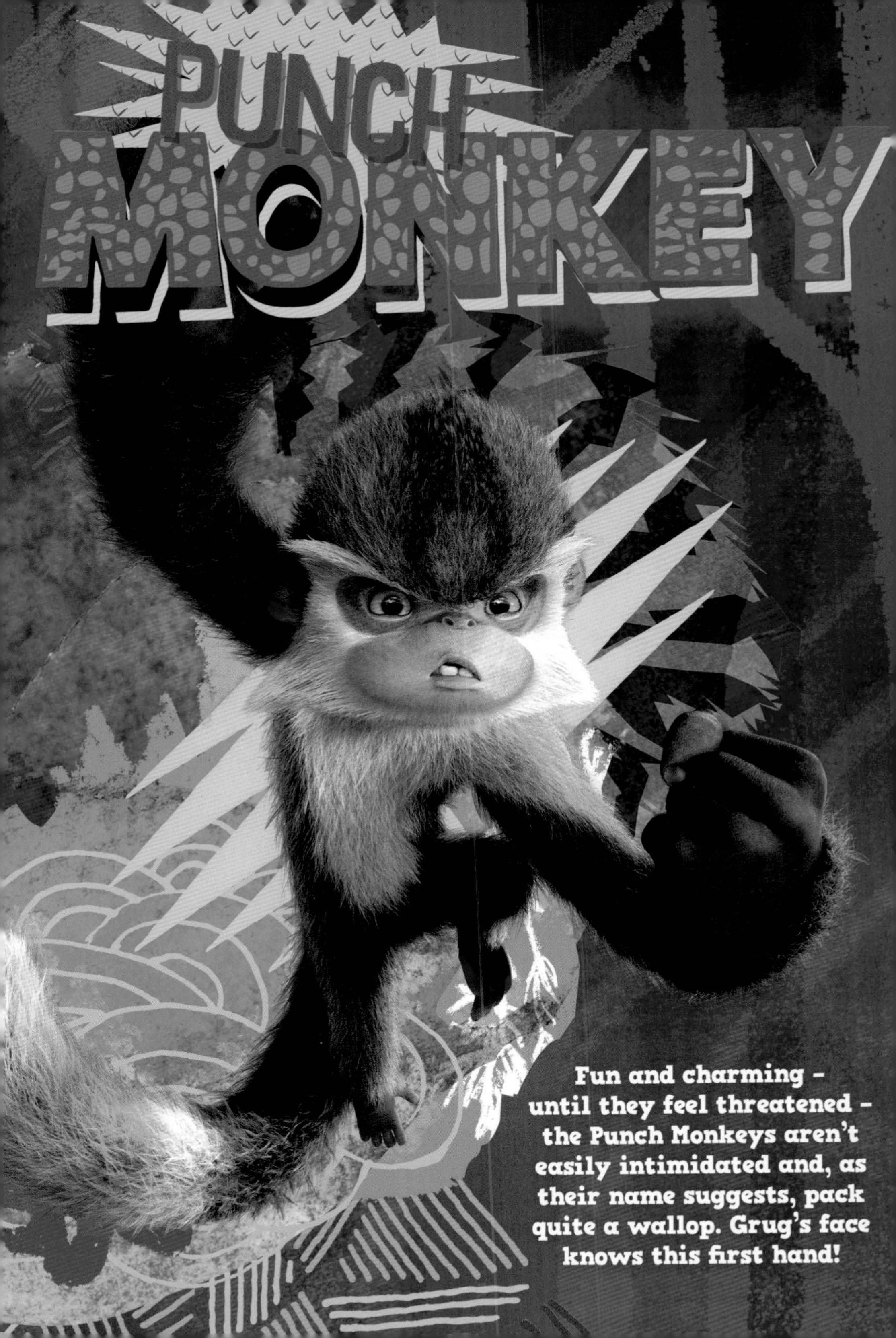

Fun and charming – until they feel threatened – the Punch Monkeys aren't easily intimidated and, as their name suggests, pack quite a wallop. Grug's face knows this first hand!

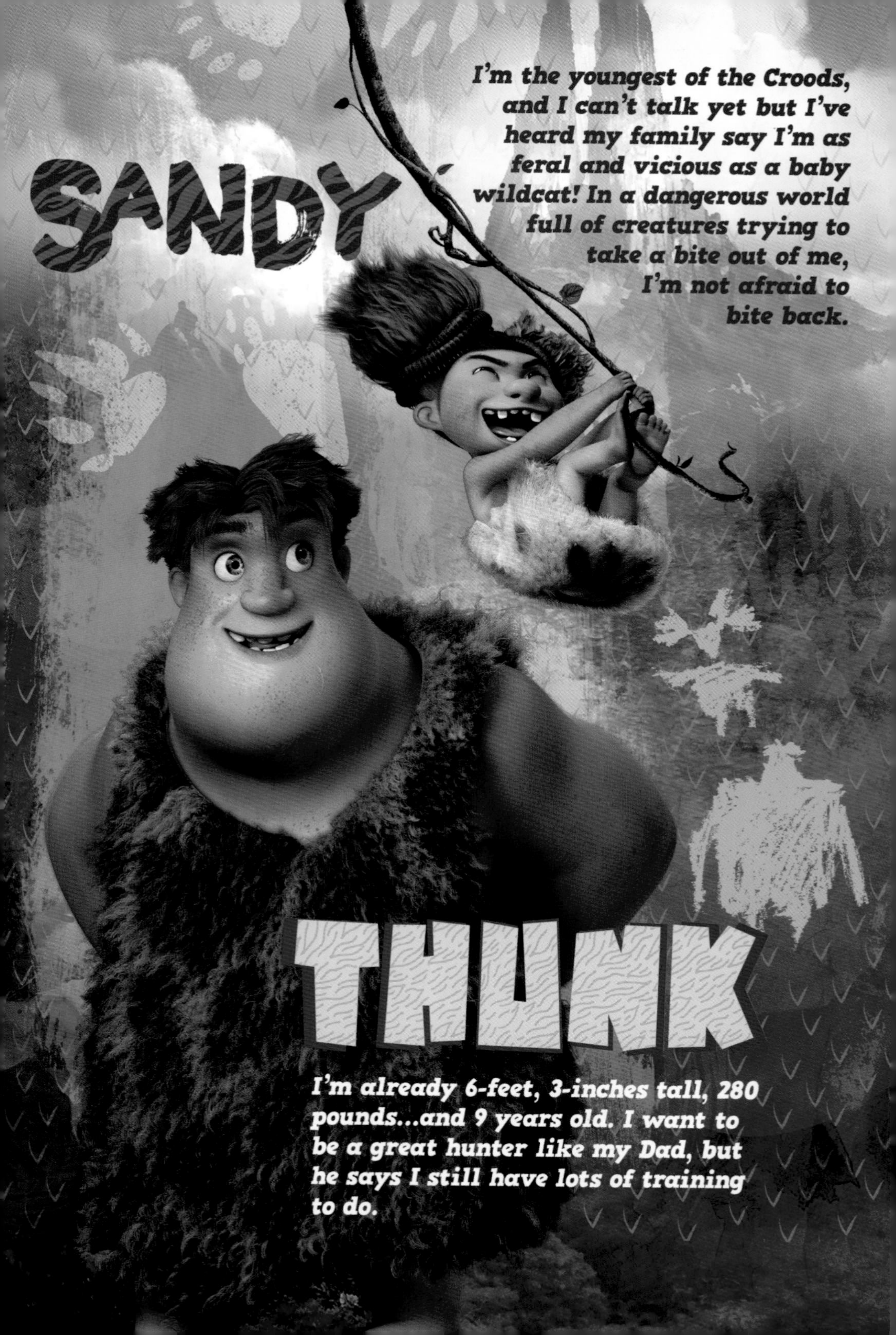

SANDY

I'm the youngest of the Croods, and I can't talk yet but I've heard my family say I'm as feral and vicious as a baby wildcat! In a dangerous world full of creatures trying to take a bite out of me, I'm not afraid to bite back.

THUNK

I'm already 6-feet, 3-inches tall, 280 pounds...and 9 years old. I want to be a great hunter like my Dad, but he says I still have lots of training to do.

GRAN

My name's Gran. I lived through the ice age. What did you do? Okay, I'm a little cranky. You'd be cranky too if you were my age. Forty-six is as old as dirt in the Croodaceous period. I've seen it all: man-eating plants, bone-crushing Macawnivores, you name it, but the thing that worries me the most is my son-in-law Grug. He'd be worthless if it weren't for me keeping him in line.

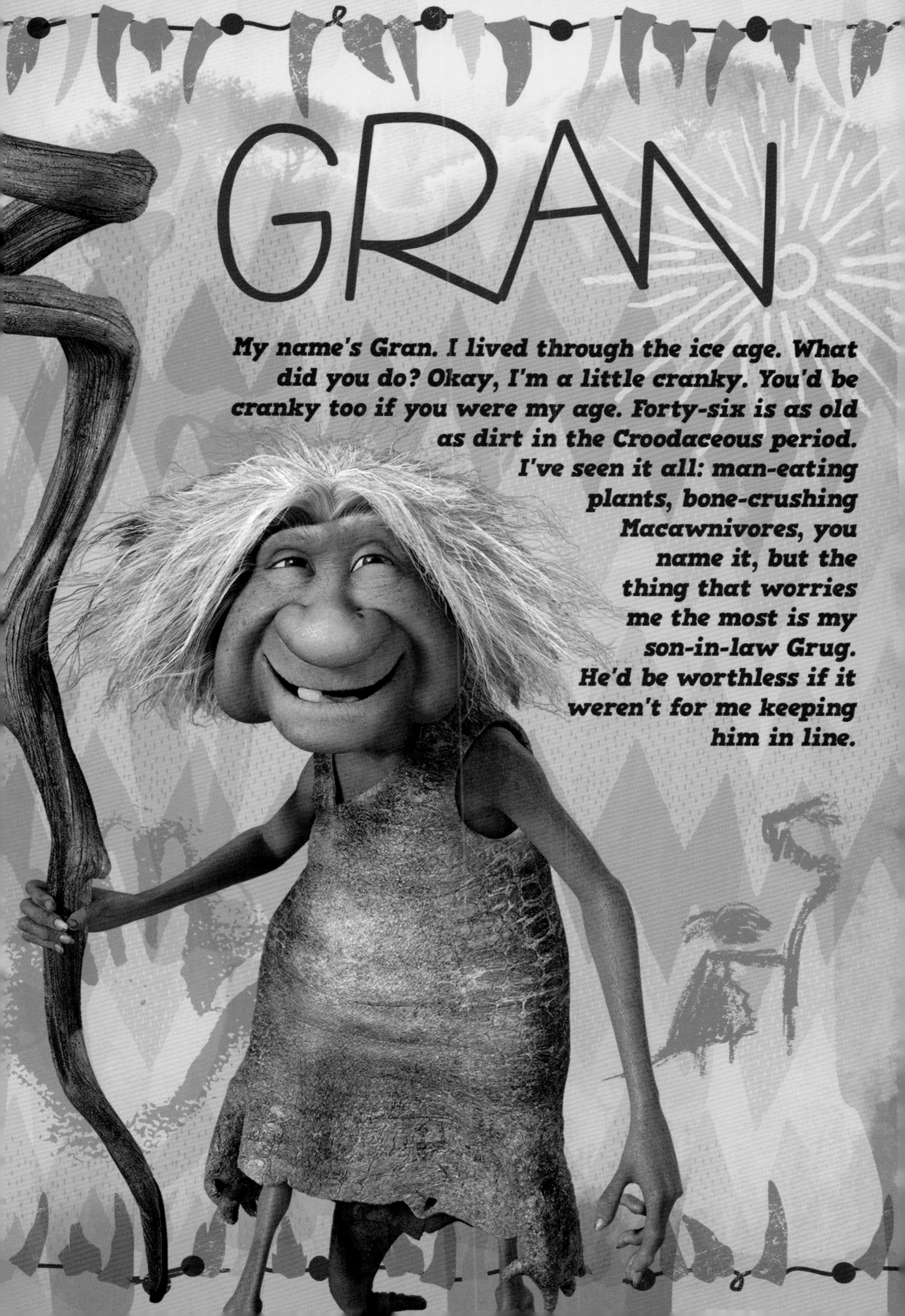

Liyote

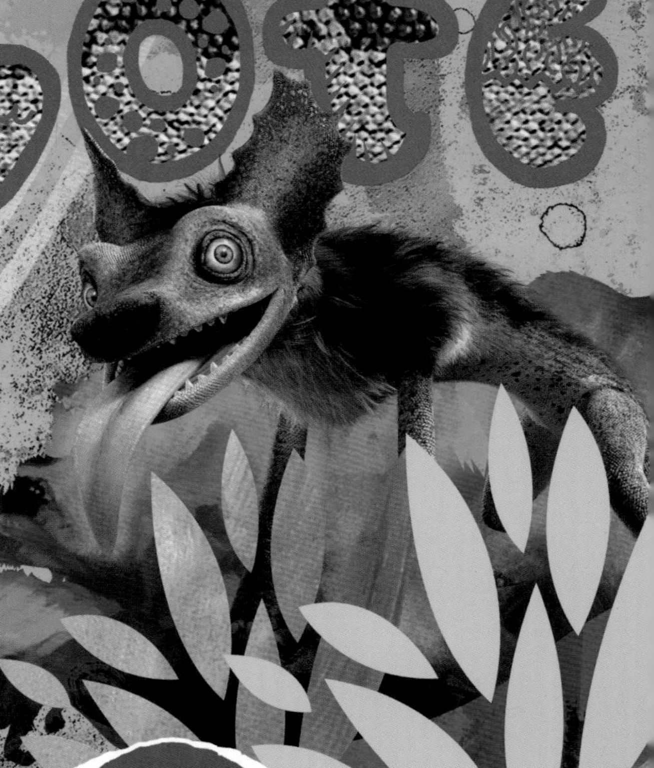

Part coyote and part lizard, these critters enjoy sunning themselves outside the Croods' cave, and are also fierce competion during the breakfast run.

Crocopup

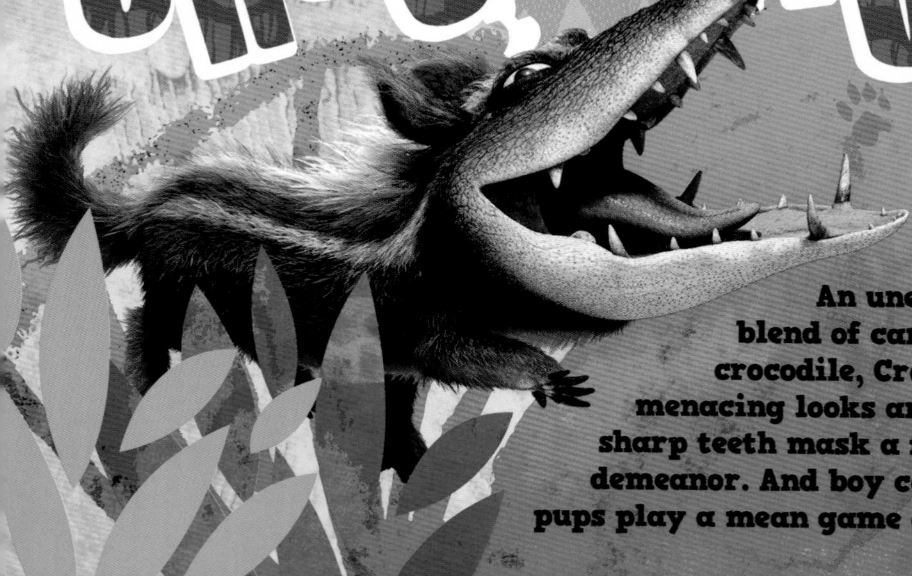

An unexpected blend of canine and crocodile, Crocopups' menacing looks and razor sharp teeth mask a friendly demeanor. And boy can these pups play a mean game of fetch.

Pack Up Your Troubles

WRITTEN BY GEORGIA BALL
ART BY NATHAN WATSON
COLORS BY ANTONIO & FERNANDO PENICHE
LETTERS BY DERON BENNETT
EDITS BY AARON SPARROW

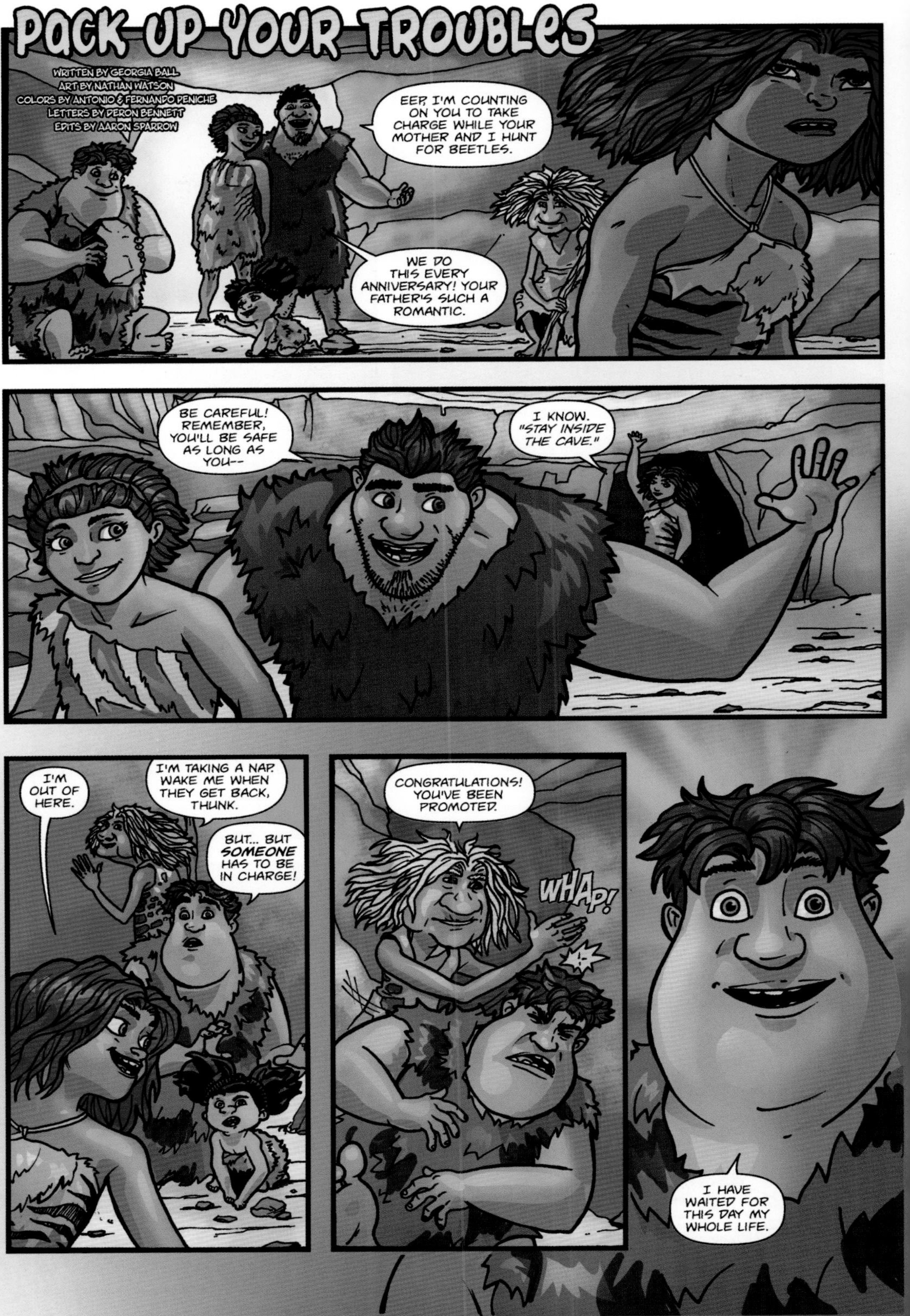
EEP, I'M COUNTING ON YOU TO TAKE CHARGE WHILE YOUR MOTHER AND I HUNT FOR BEETLES.
WE DO THIS EVERY ANNIVERSARY! YOUR FATHER'S SUCH A ROMANTIC.
BE CAREFUL! REMEMBER, YOU'LL BE SAFE AS LONG AS YOU--
I KNOW. "STAY INSIDE THE CAVE."
I'M OUT OF HERE.
I'M TAKING A NAP. WAKE ME WHEN THEY GET BACK, THUNK.
BUT... BUT SOMEONE HAS TO BE IN CHARGE!
CONGRATULATIONS! YOU'VE BEEN PROMOTED.
WHAP!
I HAVE WAITED FOR THIS DAY MY WHOLE LIFE.

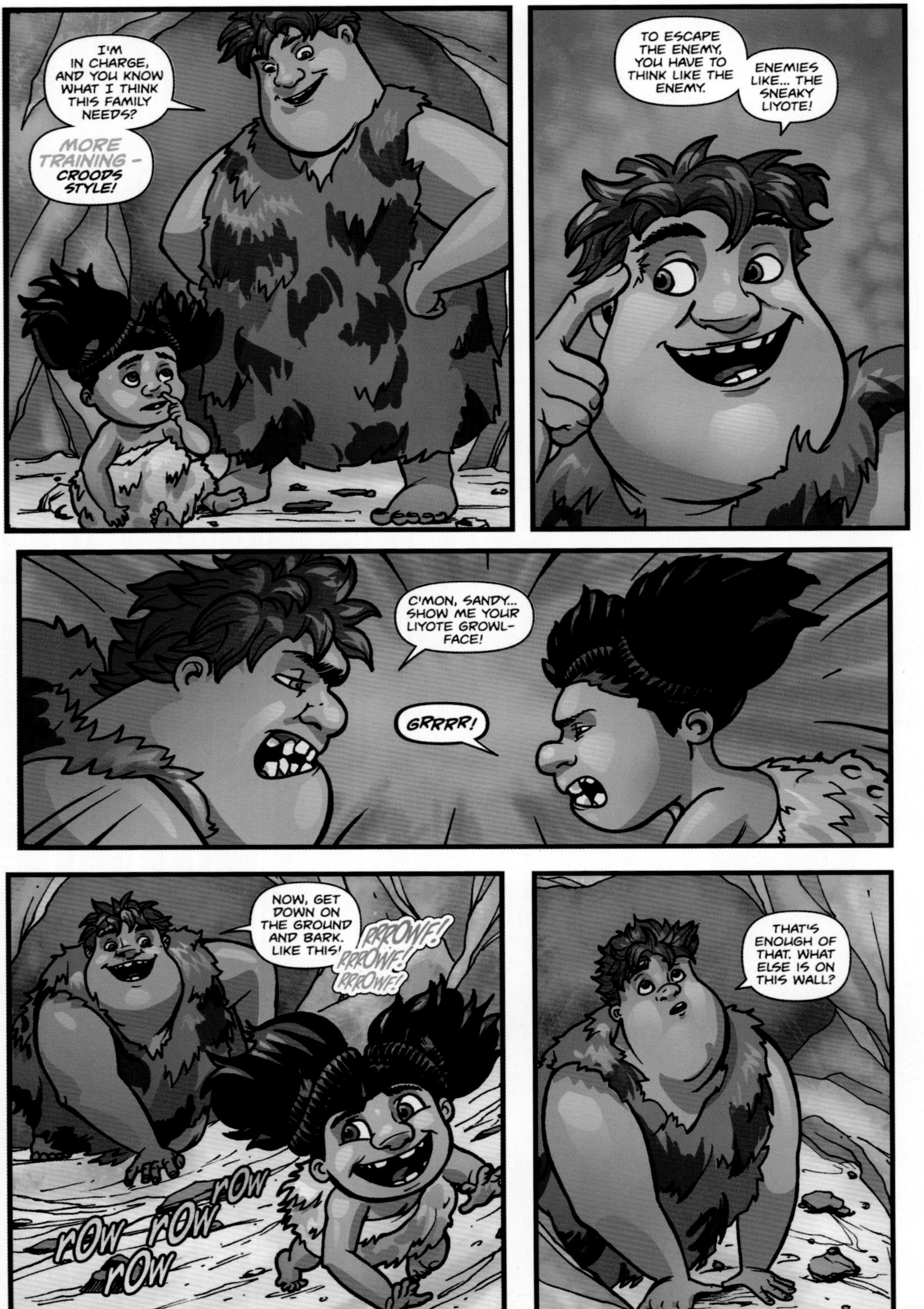
I'M IN CHARGE, AND YOU KNOW WHAT I THINK THIS FAMILY NEEDS?
MORE TRAINING - CROODS STYLE!
TO ESCAPE THE ENEMY, YOU HAVE TO THINK LIKE THE ENEMY.
ENEMIES LIKE... THE SNEAKY LIYOTE!
C'MON, SANDY... SHOW ME YOUR LIYOTE GROWL-FACE!
GRRRR!
NOW, GET DOWN ON THE GROUND AND BARK. LIKE THIS!
RRROWF! RRROWF! RRROWF!
rOw rOw rOw rOw
THAT'S ENOUGH OF THAT. WHAT ELSE IS ON THIS WALL?

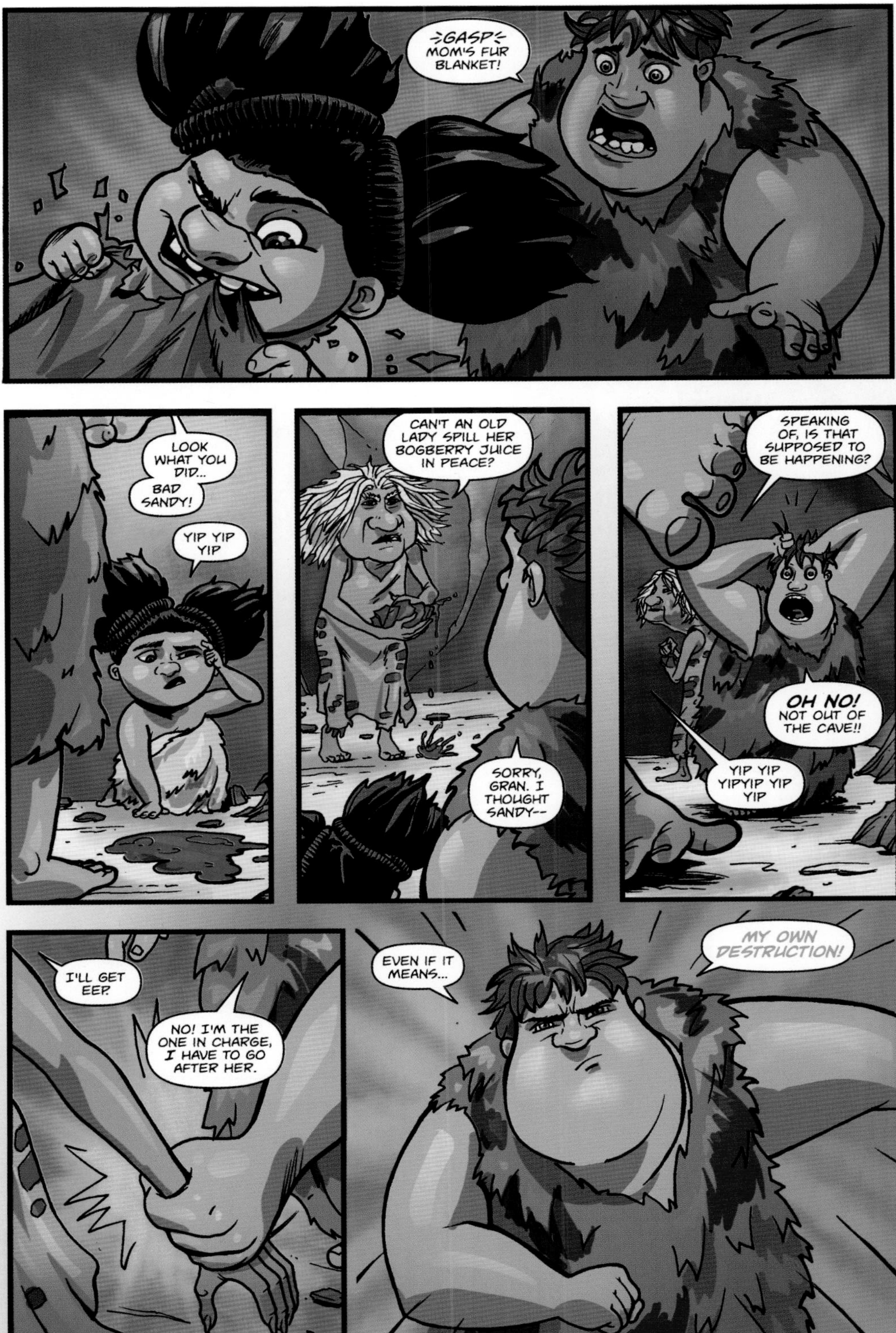

GASP
MOM'S FUR BLANKET!
LOOK WHAT YOU DID... BAD SANDY!
YIP YIP YIP
CAN'T AN OLD LADY SPILL HER BOGBERRY JUICE IN PEACE?
SORRY, GRAN. I THOUGHT SANDY--
SPEAKING OF, IS THAT SUPPOSED TO BE HAPPENING?
OH NO! NOT OUT OF THE CAVE!!
YIP YIP YIPYIP YIP YIP
I'LL GET EEP.
NO! I'M THE ONE IN CHARGE, I HAVE TO GO AFTER HER.
EVEN IF IT MEANS...
MY OWN DESTRUCTION!

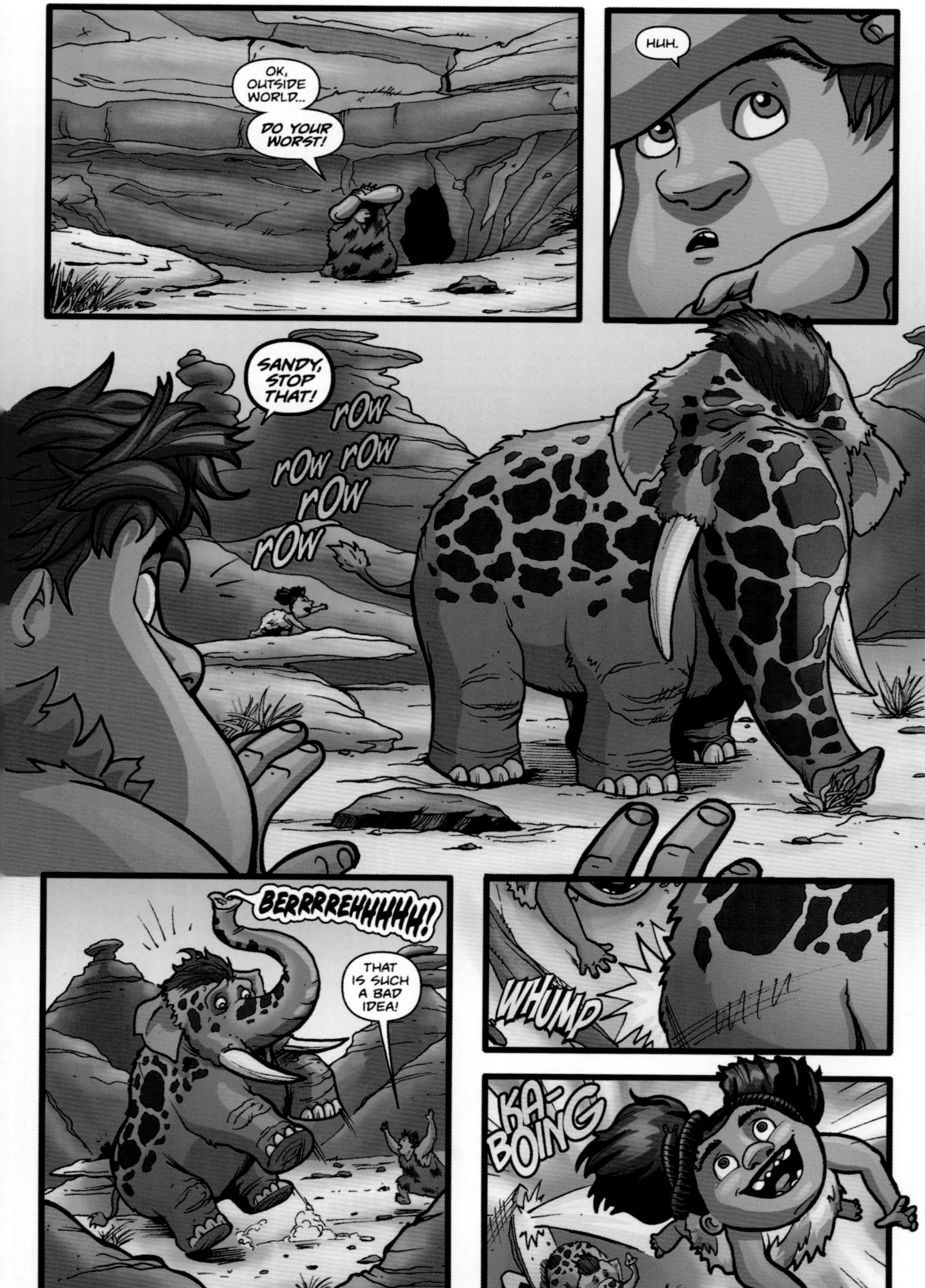
OK, OUTSIDE WORLD...
DO YOUR WORST!
HUH.
SANDY, STOP THAT!
rOw rOw rOw rOw rOw
BERRRREHHHHH!
THAT IS SUCH A BAD IDEA!
WHUMP
KA-BOING

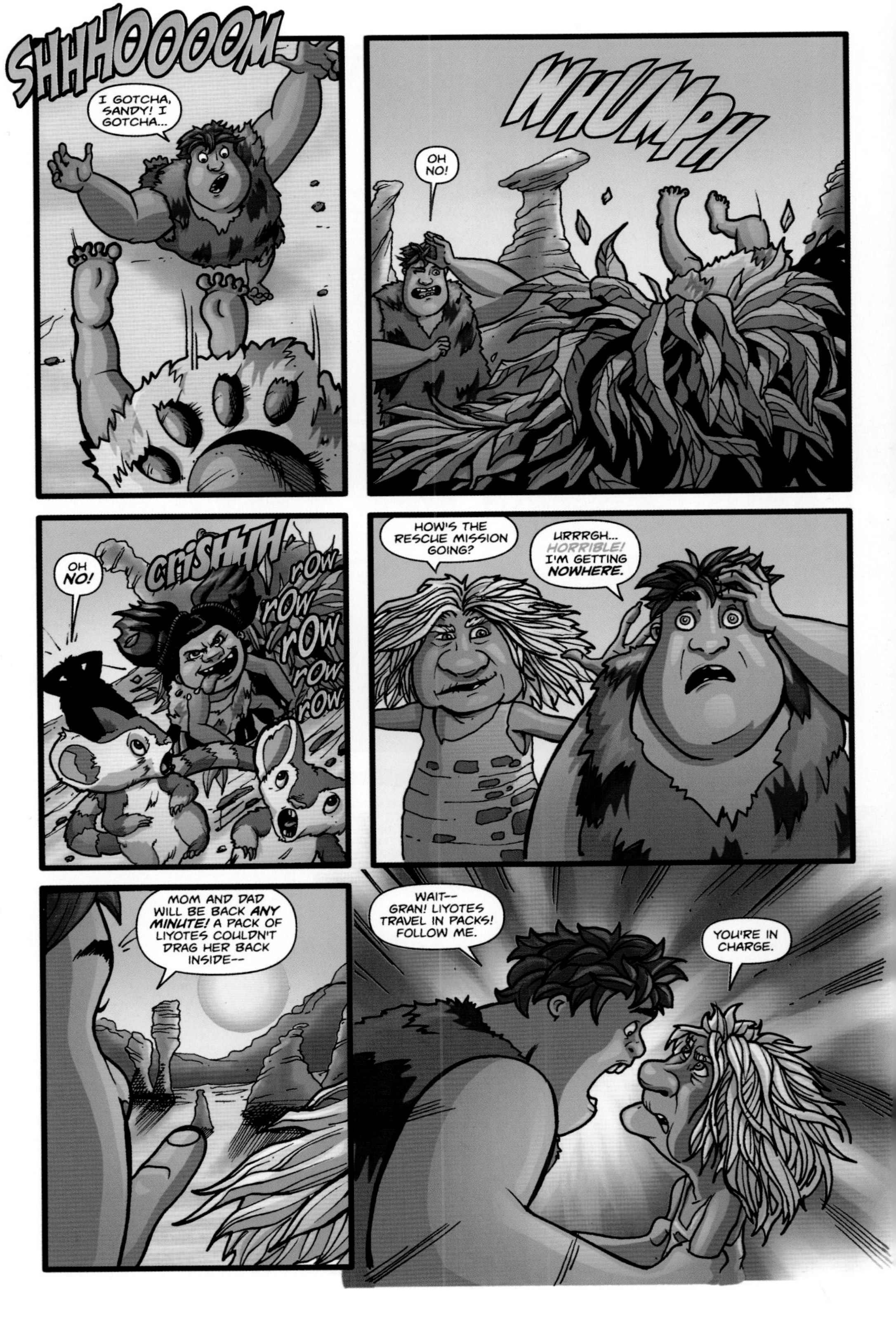
SHHHOOOOM
I GOTCHA, SANDY! I GOTCHA...
WHUMPH
OH NO!
CRiSHHH
OH NO!
rOw rOw rOw rOw rOw
HOW'S THE RESCUE MISSION GOING?
URRRGH... HORRIBLE! I'M GETTING NOWHERE.
MOM AND DAD WILL BE BACK ANY MINUTE! A PACK OF LIYOTES COULDN'T DRAG HER BACK INSIDE--
WAIT-- GRAN! LIYOTES TRAVEL IN PACKS! FOLLOW ME.
YOU'RE IN CHARGE.

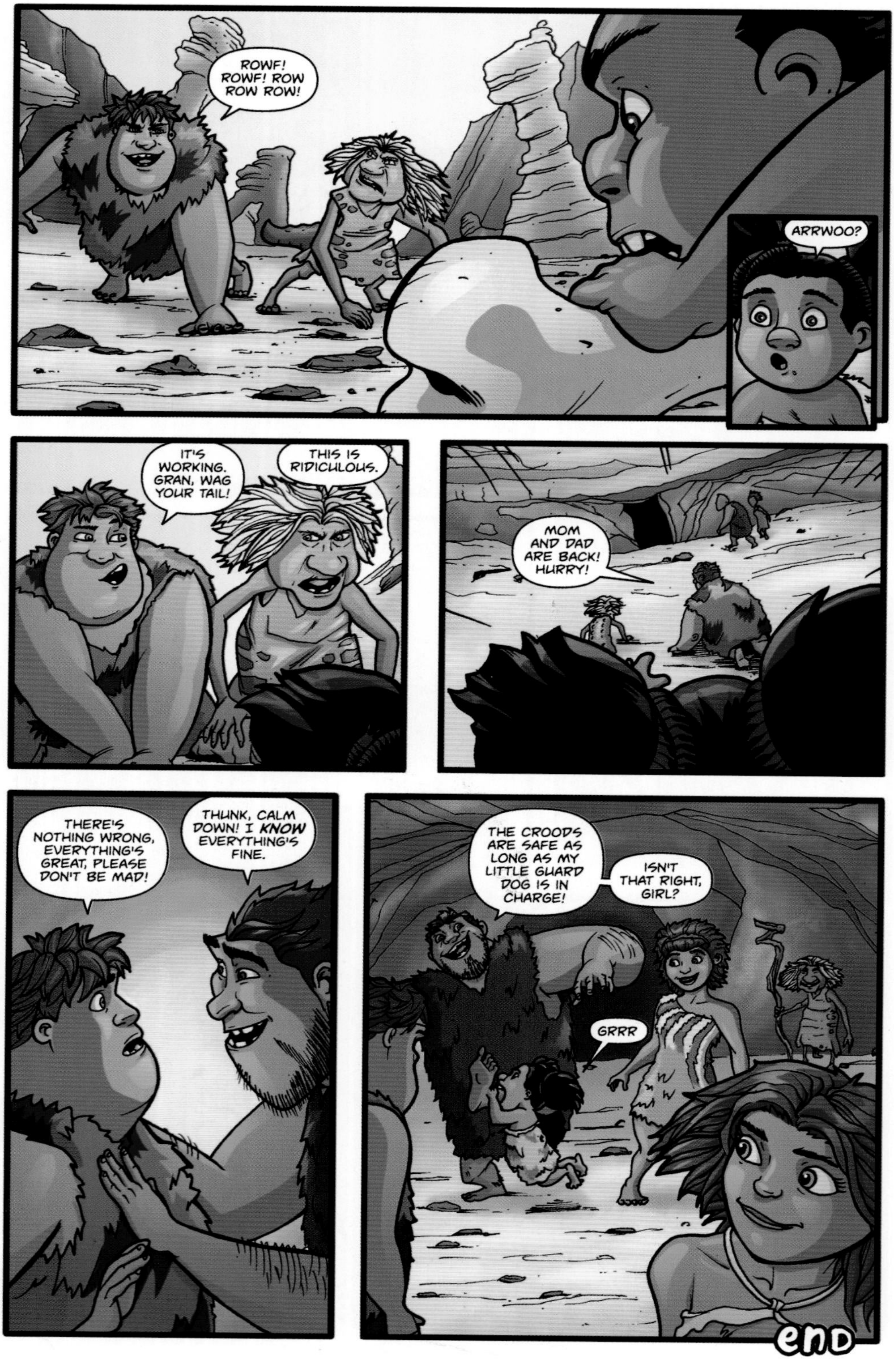
ROWF! ROWF! ROW ROW ROW!
ARRWOO?
IT'S WORKING. GRAN, WAG YOUR TAIL!
THIS IS RIDICULOUS.
MOM AND DAD ARE BACK! HURRY!
THERE'S NOTHING WRONG, EVERYTHING'S GREAT, PLEASE DON'T BE MAD!
THUNK, CALM DOWN! I KNOW EVERYTHING'S FINE.
THE CROODS ARE SAFE AS LONG AS MY LITTLE GUARD DOG IS IN CHARGE!
ISN'T THAT RIGHT, GIRL?
GRRR
end

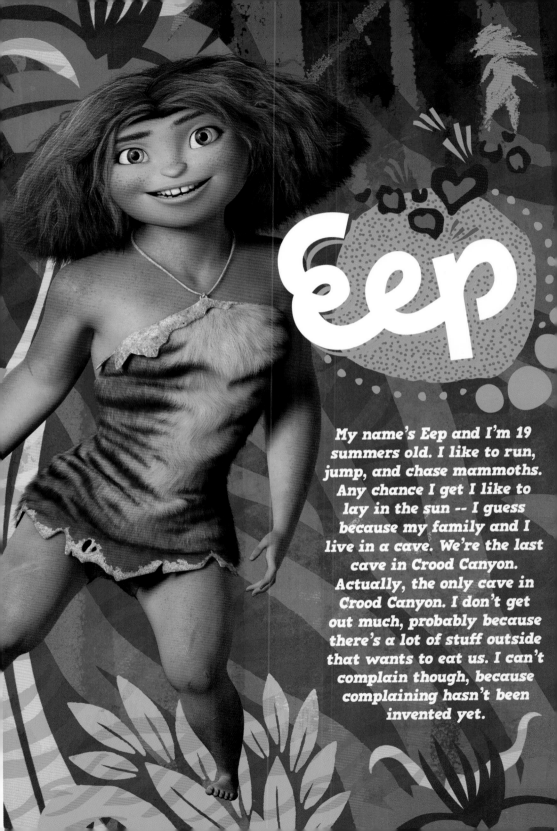

eep

My name's Eep and I'm 19 summers old. I like to run, jump, and chase mammoths. Any chance I get I like to lay in the sun -- I guess because my family and I live in a cave. We're the last cave in Crood Canyon. Actually, the only cave in Crood Canyon. I don't get out much, probably because there's a lot of stuff outside that wants to eat us. I can't complain though, because complaining hasn't been invented yet.

GUY

Hi, I'm Guy. You might say I like to travel. In fact, I've been walking alone since I was a little kid. The alone time gives me lots of time to think. Like wondering where the rain comes from and where do the suns go to sleep at night. Besides hanging out with my best friend, my pet sloth, Belt, I like coming up with ideas and inventing things. I also like hanging out with the Croods, except the times when Eep's Dad tries to kill me.

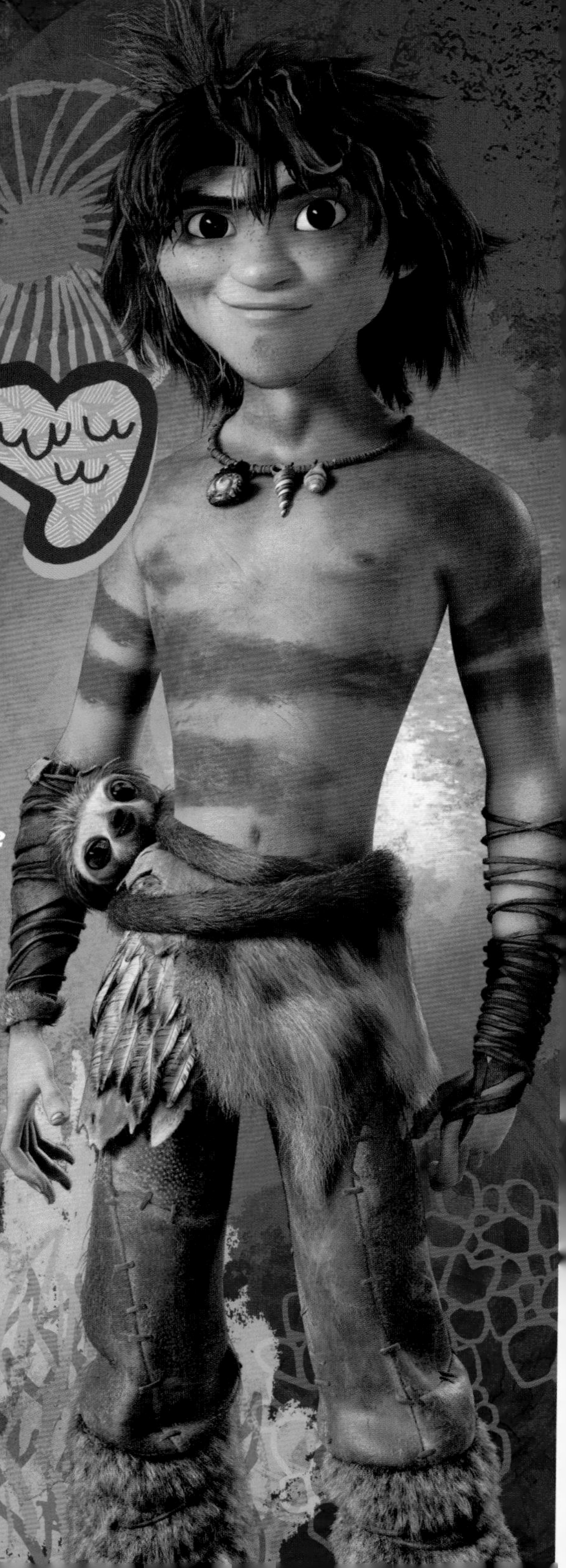

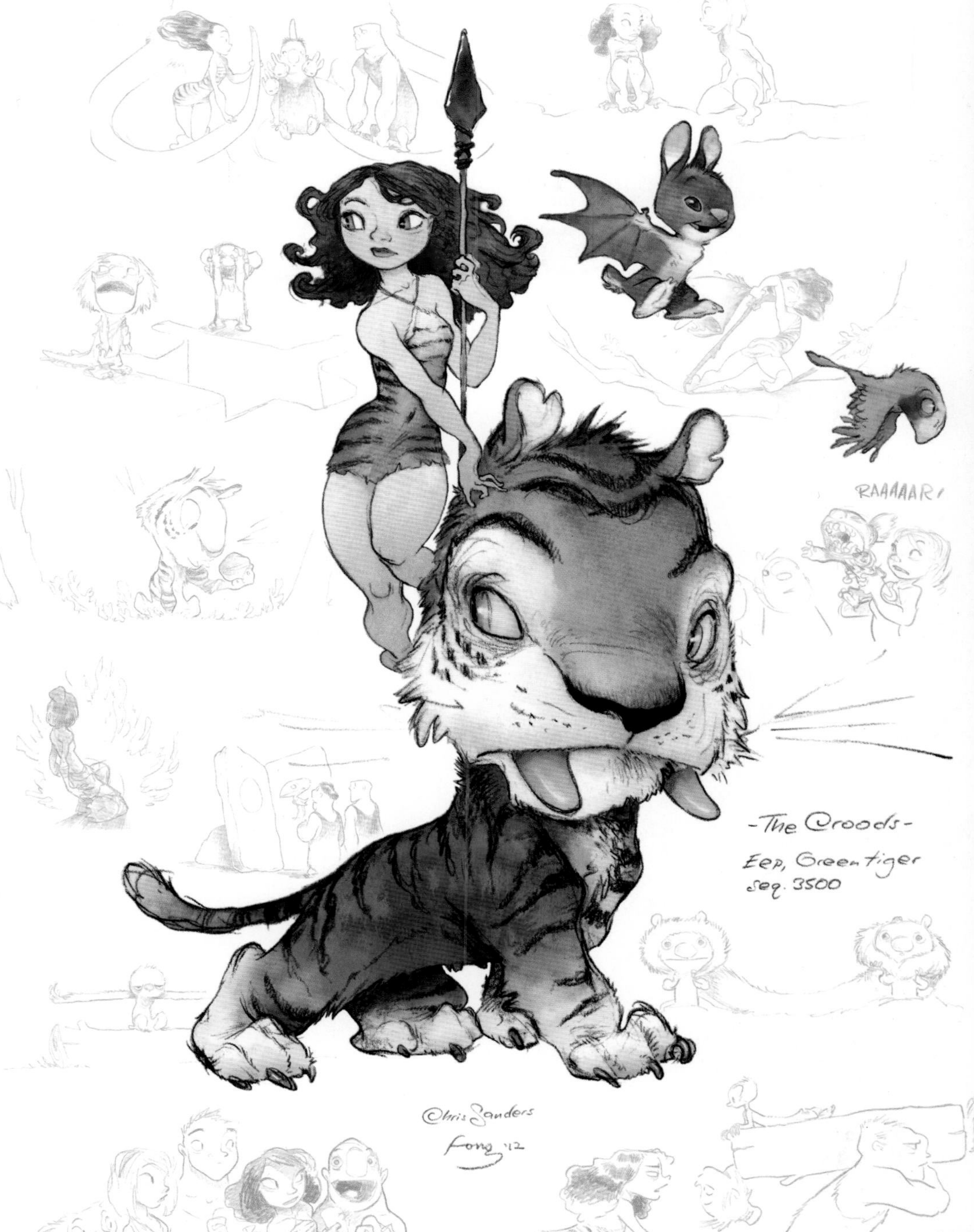

RAAAAAR!
-The Croods-
Eep, Greentiger
seq. 3500
Chris Sanders
Fong '12

Exclusive Art
Drawn By Chris Sanders and Colored By Arthur Fong

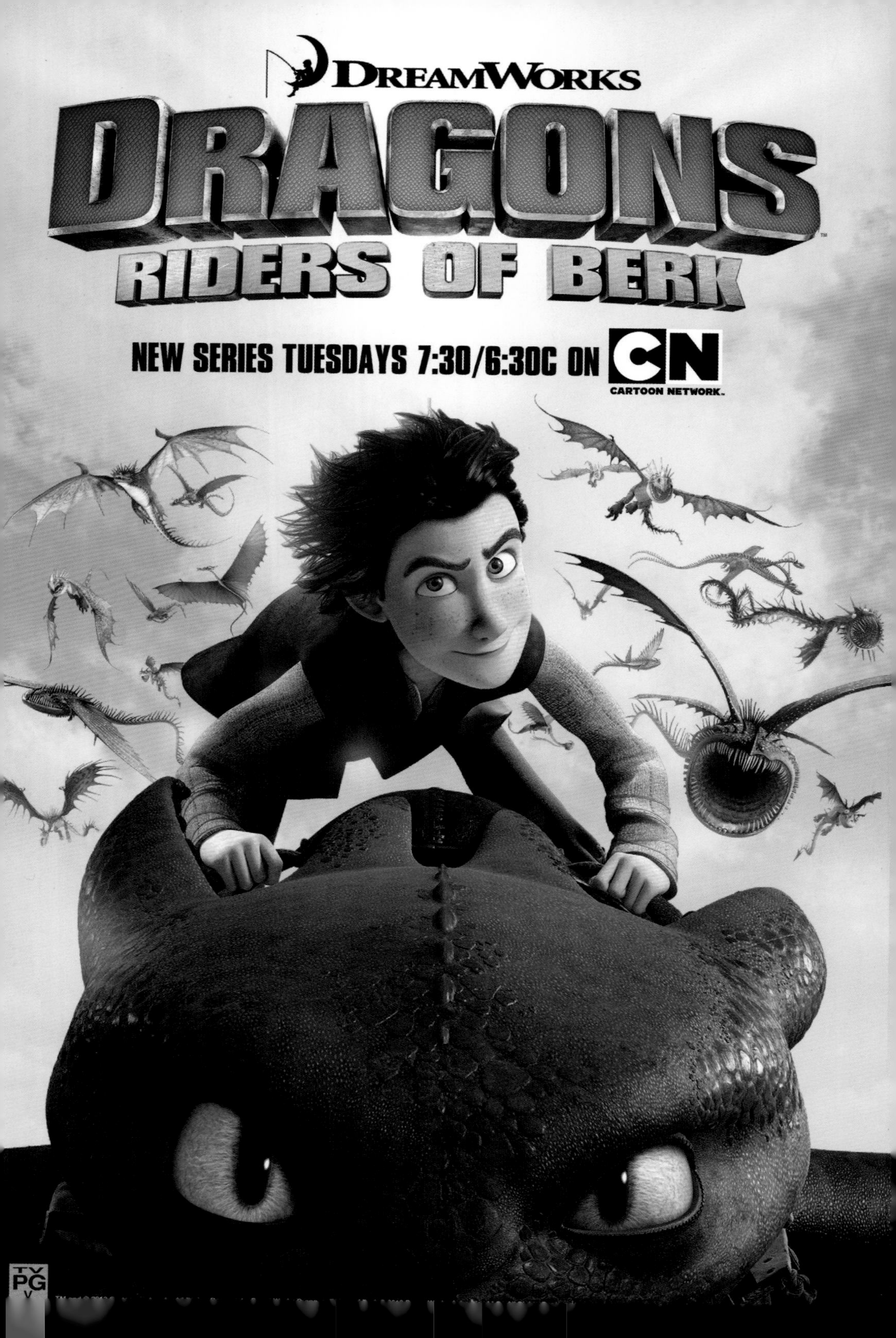
DreamWorks
DRAGONS
RIDERS OF BERK
NEW SERIES TUESDAYS 7:30/6:30C ON
CN
CARTOON NETWORK.
TV PG V

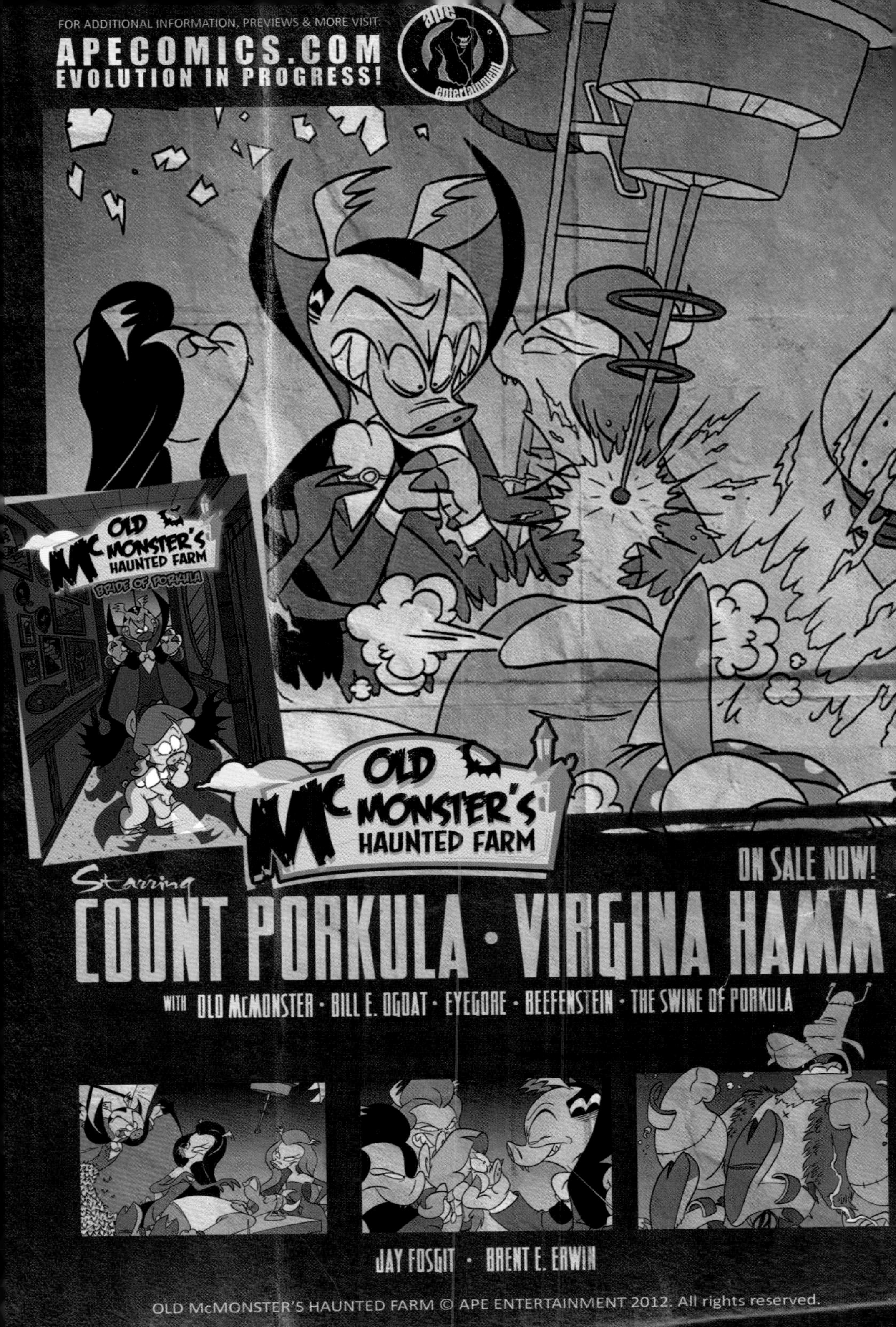
FOR ADDITIONAL INFORMATION, PREVIEWS & MORE VISIT:
APECOMICS.COM
EVOLUTION IN PROGRESS!
ape entertainment
OLD McMONSTER'S HAUNTED FARM
BRIDE OF PORKULA
OLD McMONSTER'S HAUNTED FARM
ON SALE NOW!
Starring
COUNT PORKULA · VIRGINA HAMM
WITH OLD McMONSTER · BILL E. OGOAT · EYEGORE · BEEFENSTEIN · THE SWINE OF PORKULA
JAY FOSGIT · BRENT E. ERWIN
OLD McMONSTER'S HAUNTED FARM © APE ENTERTAINMENT 2012. All rights reserved.

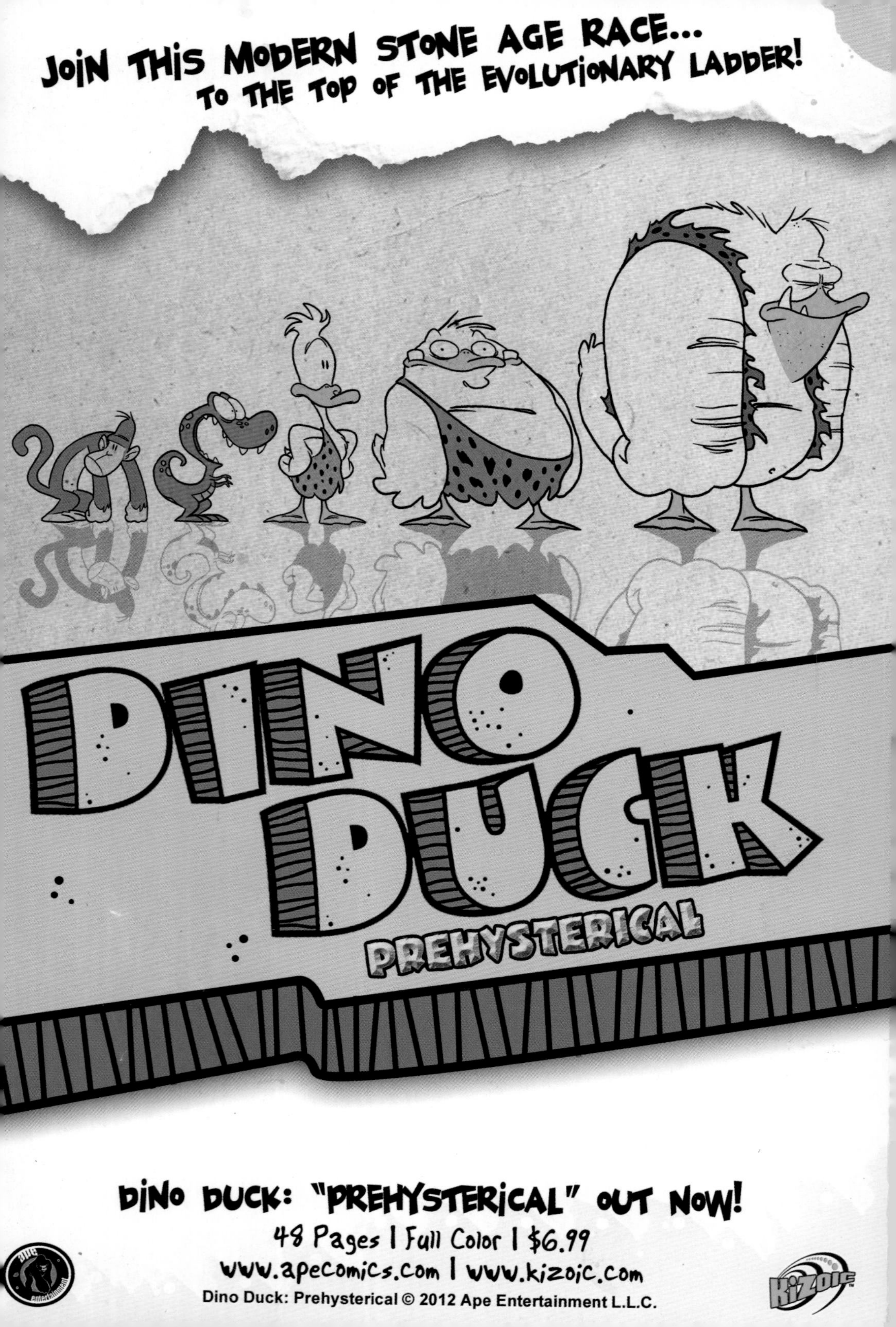
JOIN THIS MODERN STONE AGE RACE...
TO THE TOP OF THE EVOLUTIONARY LADDER!
DINO DUCK
PREHYSTERICAL
DINO DUCK: "PREHYSTERICAL" OUT NOW!
48 Pages | Full Color | $6.99
www.apecomics.com | www.kizoic.com
Dino Duck: Prehysterical © 2012 Ape Entertainment L.L.C.